*A
Harlequin
Romance*

OTHER
Harlequin Romances
by ISOBEL CHACE

THE HOSPITAL
OF FATIMA

by

ISOBEL CHACE

HARLEQUIN BOOKS   TORONTO
WINNIPEG

Original hard cover edition published in 1963
by Mills & Boon Limited.

© 1963 Isobel Chace

SBN 373-01849-3

Harlequin edition published February 1975

Printed in Canada

For

MY MOTHER —

and also for Mohammed El Ahmri

CHAPTER ONE

THE NIGHT was so black that the stars seemed doubly bright and the moon a polished silver disc suspended in the heavens. It was a warm evening and unbelievably silent except for the soft whisper of sounds that were strange to a newcomer's ear — the sound of the palm trees in the gentle breeze and the sound of a car travelling fast some distance away.

Katherine Lane walked right to the edge of the concrete apron and gazed out into the darkness beyond. If she were facing south there would be nothing but land now between her and Cape Town; miles and miles of land, the land that went to make up the great continent of Africa. Smiling a little at the thought, she turned and rejoined the group who had just left the aeroplane that stood, enormous, in one corner of the airfield. On the other side, destroying the illusion that they were alone in all Tunisia, were the airport buildings with their bright lights and restless activity.

At last the queue moved forward and it was Katherine's turn to present her passport to the vigilant official whose job it was to check and stamp it. He looked at her photograph for a long time and then looked at her.

"This is you, *mademoiselle?*" he asked, his voice tinged with disbelief.

Katherine swallowed nervously and nodded.

"Yes," she said huskily.

"*Vraiment?* I find it hard to believe! You are far more lovely than the camera would have us believe!" He stamped the open page with a firm, deliberate movement. "I hope you have a pleasant stay in our country."

Katherine accepted her passport with grateful fingers, taking an oblique look at the photograph inside. It was not very flattering, perhaps, but neither was it as bad as some she had seen of other people. It had caught that clear, wide-eyed look that had made the other nurses tease her by saying that at least she *looked* honest. It showed too the fairness of her hair that she wore in two plaits round her head because she could never quite bring herself to cut it all off. It suited her that way, though, giving her a quaint air of dignity that the responsibilities of her profession had added to, making her look a good deal more confident than she actually was. But she wasn't beautiful, she wasn't even what she would call pretty.

She put her passport carefully away in her handbag and hurried over to retrieve her luggage from the ever-growing chaos on the Customs counter.

"This is yours, *mademoiselle?*"

"Yes, all this," she replied automatically.

It was not a great deal when one considered that the two suitcases held most of her worldly possessions. It had meant paying a little in excess baggage, but Katherine had thought that it was worth it. It was the one luxury that she had allowed herself, for she still couldn't quite think of the money as being hers and, for the moment, it was quite sufficient to be going to a completely strange country in any capacity whatsoever.

The Customs official lifted his scarlet skull-cap and scratched his head thoughtfully.

"You are a doctor, perhaps?" he asked her.

Katherine smiled. Really it was too absurd to be asked all these questions, but it was nice too.

"I'm a nurse," she said.

A broad smile answered hers.

"Welcome to Tunisia!" he laughed, very much

in the grand manner, and waved to a porter to come and carry her baggage away.

"Taxi, *madame?* I find taxi while you change money, yes? No?"

"Yes," she agreed.

It was strange to stand and listen to the babble of French all around her with the harsher sounds of Arabic underneath as the porters called to one another. It was fascinating too to watch the people. A little group of veiled women huddled in a corner, and men in *djellabahs* stood gossiping in every doorway.

Perhaps it was because it was all so strange to her that she noticed when a single European walked in and went over to the Customs counter. She watched him unfold some official-looking papers and present them to a tubby little man dressed in a *burnous*.

Katherine watched him getting angrier and angrier, and wondered why. He didn't look a patient man at the best of times. His nose was too prominent and he had odd, lop-sided features that were attractive in their own way, but added to the fierce expression that his bushy eyebrows gave him. The Arab waved his hands in the air, helplessly and a little apologetically, and the man said something to him in Arabic that sounded rude even where Katherine was standing. White-faced, the official went off to confer with his colleagues and the man was left on his side of the counter, impatiently drumming his fingers on the wooden top. Then he turned and his eyes met hers.

Katherine smiled nervously and busied herself with getting out her traveller's cheques, aware that he was still staring at her. Didn't the man have any manners? she asked herself angrily. She would glower back, she thought, and then she knew she wouldn't because he looked a great deal more practised in that particular art than she would ever be.

She changed her money with a growing sense of relief and stowed the notes she had been given into her purse without pausing to count it, or even to see what it looked like. Bother the man! If there was one thing she disliked it was being made to feel self-conscious. With an effort she pulled herself together and walked slowly across to the main doors and the waiting taxi.

She was just getting into the taxi when a distraught voice called to her from behind.

"Just a moment!"

She paused, sitting down on the seat of the minute scarlet and white car, and looking out through the open door.

It was that man! With increasing indignation she glared up at him.

"Well?" she asked coldly.

The anger had gone from his face. In its place was amusement, and another expression that brought the blood coursing up into her cheeks.

"Well?" she repeated even more coldly.

He smiled.

"I believe you have an addition to your luggage," he drawled. "An addition that belongs to me."

More flustered than she would admit even to herself, she glanced wildly into the back seat at her suitcases.

"Wh-what does it look like?" she asked him.

He stood there for a moment looking down at her with that same inscrutable expression.

"I'll ask the driver," he said at last.

Katherine sat up very straight on the edge of her seat while the argument raged all round her. Suitcases were hauled out of the taxi and re-stacked neatly inside again, and all the time the men carried on a violent battle in words, their gestures becoming more and more threatening every moment.

"Why don't you look in the boot?" she suggested at last.

The taxi-driver looked at her with a dawning appreciation in his eyes. He put up a hand and banged his own head sharply. But of course, where else would it be? Now perhaps everyone would be satisfied.

The package was small and hardly seemed worth all the fuss. Katherine raised her eyebrows slightly and clutched her handbag before it fell off her knee.

"May I go now?" she asked sweetly.

The man held his package tightly, his fingers tense and excited. He had nice hands, she noticed, beautifully manicured and well under control, as though they were used to carrying out the most intricate demands he could make on them. Perhaps he was an engineer? Or something to do with irrigation? She couldn't make up her mind.

He smiled at her, his eyes lighting.

"I'm sorry to have kept you waiting," he said. "I can't understand how they allowed you to take it away with you. But there's no harm done."

He wasn't French, she decided. He had the very faintest accent, but it wasn't one that she could place. Impulsively she smiled back at him.

"Where are you going? Can I give you a lift?" she asked, and wished as promptly that she hadn't.

"No. No, I have my car. Thank you very much," he added belatedly.

He gave a slight nod to the driver and the taxi shot forward into the black night. Mysterious shapes came and went on either side, looming up out of the darkness and fading away again before Katherine could identify them. Only once was she sure that they had passed a palm tree. It was caught in the orange-yellow headlights for seconds together, looking exactly like a picture postcard, and then they swept round the corner beneath it and there was nothing but darkness once again.

Edouard de Hallet had swept into London like a tornado.

"So," he had said, "the English doctors are the best in the world! Very well then, cure me!"

And the English doctors had done their best. He had been taken to one famous nursing home after another, blood tests had been taken, other doctors had been called in, and yet nobody could really discover exactly what was the matter with him.

He was, physically, a frail old man, but one was apt to forget this when faced with his fierce and extraordinary personality. He would fix the object of his displeasure with one of his strange yellow eyes and watch them wilt before him with a contemptuous pleasure. There was only one person whom he could stand being close to him for very long, and that was the quiet, rather shy nurse they had hired for him because she spoke a smattering of French and was willing to try and use it.

The nurse had been Katherine Lane.

At first she had been frankly terrified of him, but she had soon discovered that he was lonely as well as ill, and she had done her best to include him in her own simple pleasures and had listened by the hour as he had told her of his own life. He had been a very rich man. He had properties in France and an enormous citrus farm in Tunisia, as well as half an oasis in the south of that country, where they produced some of the famous Deglats Nours dates.

"Not many men could have personally supervised so much land," he had told her proudly. "Certainly there is nobody else in my family." He had snorted angrily. "Have you written to tell them that I am dying? We may as well give them the good news as soon as possible!"

Katherine had written, but there had been no reply to her letter, and she had begun to doubt that he really did have a family at all. He was a very old man, and although he certainly had a great deal of money, who knew how many of his more or less incredible stories were no more than a figment of his imagination?

It had been sad though, when he had died and there had been none but herself to mourn for him. His body had been shipped back to France to rest in his family's vault and Katherine had found herself a new job, nursing a young man who had jumped out of his aeroplane without a parachute and had, somehow, survived the incident.

It had been all of six months later when Katherine had received a letter from a firm of solicitors in London. If she would call, she had been told, they had something to tell her regarding the estate of the late Monsieur Edouard de Hallet. She had been oddly touched to think that he had left her some memento, but it had turned out to be rather more than that. He had left her the whole of his Tunisian property on the condition that she lived in that country for at least nine months in every year!

They drove into Tunis down a broad highway, lit on either side by the very latest in street lights. The approach was intersected by several other roads, and at the last of the junctions was a large round-about planted solidly with flowers that looked weird and ghostly in the fluorescent light.

"You said the Hotel Maghreb?" the taxi-driver confirmed.

Katherine nodded.

"They told me in London I could get a room for the night there." She hesitated. "Is it — is it a good hotel?" she asked him. She didn't like to tell him of her secret fear that uninvited animal life would be sharing her bed. She was prepared for almost anything in her new life, but that —! She gave a little shudder.

13

"Very nice hotel," he reassured her. "Very central."

He set the taxi straight at a small gap in the traffic and cleared it with only a couple of inches on either side. In a few seconds he had shot round another corner and braked violently outside the imposing entrance to the hotel.

"Shall I carry your bags in for you?"

Katherine thanked him. She stared up at the sky-high frontage of the hotel with the occasional chinks of light showing through the tightly shuttered windows. It smelt faintly of distemper and orange-blossom as the street smelt of traffic, woollen clothes and doughnuts. It was a warm, welcoming smell, and, straightening her shoulders, she walked up the marble steps and into the hotel.

It had once been a French hotel, though now the receptionist was a Berber with the deeper tan of the south and the manager was a tall, dignified young Arab who had taken his training in Paris and was adhering closely to the high standards he had been taught there.

Katherine went straight to the desk.

"You have a reservation for me," she said in French. "Miss Lane."

"But yes. Will you go up to your room now, or will you have dinner first?"

Katherine hadn't considered it before, but now she found she was very hungry indeed.

"I think I'll go straight in to dinner," she said.

He pulled her suitcases forward and sent them upstairs with a porter, giving his instructions in the harsher tones of Arabic and then turned easily back to French as he directed her to the dining-room.

It was a large room, completely white except for the vivid splash of orange of the curtains, picked up again in the small bowls of marigolds that stood on every table. Katherine stood for an instant in the doorway before the head waiter saw her and led her to a small table. At the same moment another man rose and came towards her. He was obviously French, with his hair cut short and the quiet, elegant movements of his hands, but it was his eyes that she noticed in particular. They were of the brightest blue that she had ever seen.

"I imagine that you must be Miss Lane?" he asked her lazily.

"Yes, I am." She sounded surprised and that made him smile.

"I am Guillaume de Hallet." He bowed slightly. "Old Edouard's nephew."

She was shocked.

"His *nephew?*" she repeated.

He looked a trifle mocking.

"Do you mean you did not know?" he asked her. "There are two of us. Myself and my sister, Chantal."

"But I wrote to you," she began, "and you didn't —"

"Didn't what? Didn't answer? How were we to know that he was really ill?"

Katherine's outraged glance met his. How very blue his eyes were! Periwinkle blue!

"You could have made inquiries!" she said coldly.

He laughed a trifle ruefully.

"How wise you are, Miss Lane," he mocked her. "Not only could but *should* have made inquiries, it seems! However, I have not come over to quarrel with you. I came to ask you if you would join us at our table. It will be better all round if we are seen to be friendly, don't you think?"

Katherine's eyes widened with dismay.

"I never dreamed he really did have any close relatives," she said miserably. "He was always so alone."

Guillaume de Hallet took her hand in his.

"That is past," he said authoritatively. "It does not do to dwell too much on these things. We must think of the future, and your life here among us in this new country."

She rose a little uncertainly. He had sounded kind —and yet there was a kind of menace behind his words. What was there to think about? She had to live on one or other of the two estates for nine months of the year, and that was that. His blue eyes smiled at her and she smiled back. She was being too imaginative, she thought, he was only trying to be kind.

Chantal de Hallet greeted her with a smile. She wore a dress of blue wild silk that fitted her like a glove and was smart in the way that only a French-woman — and a very rich Frenchwoman at that — ever could be. She too had her brother's blue eyes, but with her the blue was paler, like cloth that had been faded in the sun, and her other features were not so well put together.

"Welcome to Tunisia, Miss Lane," she said dryly. "We heard you would be arriving today."

Guillaume held out a chair and Katherine sat down on it, wishing now that she had taken the trouble to change before she had come into dinner. That wild silk took some living up to, and her own neat grey linen dress was not the answer.

"It's very kind of you to ask me over," she said quickly. "I hope I shan't keep you waiting too long for your next course."

The French girl shrugged.

"We have only just begun," she said indifferently.

So, Katherine thought, not without exasperation, it had not been Chantal's idea that she should be asked over. She wished she could like the other girl, but that ultra-smart, cold exterior was not very en-couraging.

Her soup was brought and she picked up a spoon thoughtfully.

"Do you both live in Tunisia?" she asked.

There was a moment's silence while Chantal fingered her collar restively and Guillaume pretended he hadn't heard the question.

"What did she say?" Chantal asked at last of her brother in French.

"She asked us where we lived, *chérie.*" He laughed without any amusement. "We live, my dear Miss Lane, with you. We have lived with our uncle ever since we were small children, and I imagine that you would not be so unkind as to turn us out of our home now?"

Katherine took a quick, shocked breath.

"But didn't he leave you *anything?*" she asked. Chantal looked bored.

"He left me the French estates," Guillaume said uncomfortably. "But unfortunately I do not enjoy living in France. To Chantal —" he glanced at his sister — "he left nothing at all. It is sad, *hein,* that he should have been so lacking in gratitude when she has kept his house so well all these years?"

Katherine put her spoon down again, her hunger gone.

"But that's dreadful!" she exclaimed. "Of course you must continue to live exactly as you did before! It will — it will be rather fun in a way. I've never had a proper home of my own before and I expect I have a lot to learn about such things."

Chantal smiled briefly.

"We cannot be good at everything," she said obliquely.

Katherine flushed. How could she live with her? she wondered. But she was used to hiding her emotions and making the best of the circumstances in which she found herself. The other girl would undoubtedly be out a great deal, and she herself could always retire to her room. But she wished it didn't have to be this way. She would have liked to have had a friend of her own age and sex in this strange land.

"Be quiet, Chantal!" Guillaume put in angrily. "It is not kind to antagonise Miss Lane!"

Chantal made a face at him.

"Are you so worried about your soft berth already?" she asked him sweetly. "You need not be. Miss Lane will never turn us out. She knows very well that that is not what Uncle Edouard intended at all. Besides," and an odd smile of satisfaction lit her beautifully made-up face, "it is so uncomfortable to live in a foreign country without any friends." She turned and faced Katherine squarely, her eyes contemptuous. "Isn't it, Kat'rine?"

The mocking mispronunciation of her name brought the point home to the English girl. Here she was not even Katherine, she was some foreigner named Katrine — was that how she had said it? — and she was dependent on these two for introducing her to the local Europeans, whom they had known since they were children, but who would only know her as a stranger, perhaps an interloper. She grew cold at the thought.

"No," she said, "I shall not turn you out." But she too had a temper and she hoped very much that she was not going to lose it. There would be something rather satisfactory about allowing hot, angry words to spill out over that cold, smart face — satisfactory, but dangerous. She had to live in Tunisia. Whatever happened she had to remember that.

Guillaume's blue eyes danced, meeting hers in a joke that she hadn't seen, but she liked the warm feeling it gave her. He, at least, was not her enemy.

"We are travelling to Hammamet tomorrow," he told her. "Why don't you come with us? There is plenty of room in my car."

She was grateful to him. It would be so much nicer to arrive in a party and not to have to find her own way around the estate.

"I should like that," she said shyly. "Thank you very much."

He went on to tell her about the orchards. The oranges were just beginning to ripen and the first of the fruit was being picked while the late blossom still filled the air with its fragrance. The lemons and the grapefruit came just that little bit later, but it was already possible to pick them off the trees and crush them then and there for drinks. She had come at the best time of the year, when it was not too hot, and when the whole of the neighbouring countryside was covered in a carpet of wild flowers that had to be seen to be believed.

"It sounds like Paradise," Katherine laughed.

Guillaume's eyes slid on to his sister's face.

"Or the original Garden of Eden," he said dryly.

They had almost finished dinner when the man came in. Katherine knew the instant he crossed the threshold, despite the fact that the door was behind her. She knew it by the sudden glint in Chantal's eyes and the way her hand went up automatically to straighten her hair.

Guillaume grinned and turned in his chair to see who the newcomer was.

"Ah! Dr. Kreistler!" he murmured. "That explains it."

"Explains what?" his sister asked crossly.

"Nothing," he retorted maddeningly. "Nothing at all."

Katherine glanced over her shoulder and saw him, recognising him immediately, for he was none other than the man at the airport.

"Kreistler," she repeated, turning the name over in her mind. "Is he a German?"

Guillaume shook his head.

"It sounds German, but actually he's Hungarian. He's a refugee from the 1956 uprising. He first came to Tunisia under the auspices of the World Health Organisation and he stayed on. At present he's in charge of the government hospital at Sidi Behn Ahmed."

"Sidi Behn Ahmed?"

"Isn't that —"

"Your oasis?" he smiled. "That's right. He's a big man down there. Even Uncle Edouard treated him with a proper respect!"

Chantal gave him an impatient look.

"You will excuse me, I'm sure," she said hurriedly. "It is so long since I saw the doctor." For an instant she looked almost lovely as she rose to her feet. "I must see him now," she added abruptly, and hurried across the dining-room to his table.

She came up behind him and blew softly on the back of his head. Katherine saw him rise quickly to greet her. He looked pleased to see her and his smile was indulgent as he pulled out a chair for her. It was so silly to feel resentful, but somehow Katherine had been regarding him as her own personal find, and it hurt her to think that he also was a friend of the de Hallets, and had been long before she had ever met him.

She tore her attention back to Guillaume.

"Does he come up to Tunis often?" she asked.

"He comes up for medical supplies at intervals," he replied. Sardonic amusement spread across his face. "He comes also to see Chantal," he added. "She regards him very much as her property, and she is a girl who knows very well how to look after her own."

Katherine didn't doubt him for a moment. She could feel the warm, rich colour creeping up her cheeks and it made her more than a little cross.

"I saw him at the airport," she said unnecessarily. "That was why I was interested."

Guillaume raised one expressive eyebrow. He still looked amused, but he looked a little sorry for her as well.

"So?" was all he said.

CHAPTER TWO

THE INSTANT that Katherine awoke she knew that she was no longer in England. There was a quality in the hot sunshine that she had never seen before and the noises coming up from the busy street below sounded strange and yet, in an odd way, also familiar. She went over to the window and pushed back the shutters, gazing down at the scene below her. There was a man selling sweetmeats on the corner and a group of veiled women giggling among themselves as they passed him. Katherine watched them with a rising sense of excitement, suddenly anxious to hurry out and explore all she could in the short morning that she had at her disposal. Guillaume had said they would be setting out for Hammamet straight after lunch, but she had all of three — she glanced at her watch — no, four hours before she need meet the de Hallets at the entrance of the hotel.

She dressed quickly, taking advantage of the shower in her room, and packed her bags before she left so that she would have less to do when she came back. In less than a quarter of an hour she was ready and made her way downstairs to the dining-room for breakfast.

It was practically empty when she went in, with only a few tables laid up at the far end. She chose a table, and was on the point of sitting down when she saw Dr. Kreistler coming towards her.

"Do you mind if I share your table?" he asked her.

She smiled up at him.

"Of course not."

He sat down and signalled to the waiter to bring them both some coffee.

"I had not realised at the airport yesterday that

you were the Miss Lane we have been waiting for so long. I hope you are not up so early because you couldn't sleep?"

"Oh, no! I slept very well." She bit her lip. It was not often that she wanted to impress anyone, but there was something about this man that made her want him to like her. She wanted it so much that it gave her a funny, tight feeling round her middle and made her nervous.

He smiled at her and she found herself smiling back.

"That is good," he said. "I am told you have the whole morning to yourself? Perhaps you will allow me to show you something of Tunis?"

She chuckled.

"I'd love it!" she said frankly. "If you're sure you can spare the time? I shouldn't like to impose —"

"I have the time," he replied.

She spread her roll thickly with butter and apricot jam and prepared to enjoy it. For the moment she was completely happy and it showed in the slight sparkle in her eyes and the way that her mouth couldn't quite stop smiling.

"How big is your hospital?" she asked him.

He seemed surprised that she should ask. His eyebrows flew up, and though he quickly veiled his astonishment, for an instant it was plain in his eyes.

"We have about fifty beds in the main block," he told her. "There is a smaller eye hospital also, though in the last few years we have practically got on top of trachoma. One can still see children who have had the beginnings of it, though. At best it leaves a terrible squint, at worst the patient becomes completely blind. There is still a great deal of work to be done in the more backward areas."

Katherine's quick sympathy was caught.

"And do the parents co-operate by bringing their children in to the clinics?" she asked.

He laughed.

"Oh yes, they come! They come from curiosity if for no other reason."

Katherine's eyes sparkled.

"I should love to see it all!" she exclaimed on a sigh.

"If you come to Sidi Behn Ahmed I shall show you around," he offered. "But I doubt that you will come. It is too hot in the south for people like you."

"Like me?" She was hurt, and it showed in the sudden quiver of her lips.

His face hardened and his eyes were grey and remote.

"We all work at the oasis," he said abruptly. "We would not have the time to entertain you properly. You will do better to stay at Hammamet with Chantal and be amused by the quaint customs of the country."

The piece of roll she was eating grew dry and tasteless.

"And what gave you the right to be so superior, Dr. Kreistler?" she asked in dangerously quiet tones.

He reached across the table and picked up one of her hands in his.

"This, Miss Lane?" he suggested. He ran his thumb down the edge of her forefinger with a slight smile. "They are lovely hands, but they do not bear the marks of toil!"

Katherine froze. The touch of his hand on hers had done odd things to her breathing and she was so indignant that she could hardly speak.

"I look after my hands!"

His smile grew until it reached right up into his eyes.

"I'm sure you do," he agreed indulgently. He put her hand back on her side of the table with gentle fingers. "They are active hands as well as being pretty. Do you play the piano?"

"No, I do not!" she said crossly.

He shrugged slightly, dismissing the matter.

"Have you finished your coffee?" he asked her. "Shall we go?"

She rose and followed him out of the dining-room, still fuming at his stupid, arrogant superiority. A doctor should know better than to jump to such conclusions, she thought angrily. And why those particular conclusions? Did she *look* as though she had been living in the lap of luxury ever since she had been born?

They were selling flowers in the Avenue Habib Bourguiba. The central pavement, lined with thick, shady trees to keep off the sun, was massed with blooms of every colour and variety. There were marigolds and orange-blossom, daffodils and tulips, wild gladioli and bougainvillea, already drooping in the hot atmosphere. Katherine hesitated and then stood stock-still in the middle of the stalls, savouring the sweet perfume and the harsh cries of the sellers.

"You would like some flowers?" Dr. Kreistler asked her, smiling down at her bright fair hair. The neat, prim way that she wore it was so at odds with the temper he had seen reflected in her eyes and the easy laughter that came to her lips.

"They would die long before we could get them home," she said regretfully. "It doesn't seem possible, does it, at this time of year?"

He stood aside for a man to pass him.

"Why not at this time of the year? Later on it will be too hot. Now is the best time." He picked up a single blossom and fastened it to her collar, flicking a small coin to the owner of the stall. "You have forgiven me for whatever I said that annoyed you so, no?"

"There was nothing to forgive," she said stiffly. She smelt the bloom timidly. It was yellow and she did not know its name, but its scent was familiar, soft and clinging and — *expensive!* Her eyes swept up to meet his, wide and innocent. "Was there, Dr. Kreistler?"

To her surprise he laughed.

"You're not at all what I was led to expect somehow," he said. "Just what were you to Edouard de Hallet?"

I was his *nurse!* That was what she should have told him. But she was too proud. It seemed to her that Chantal had done all the telling that was necessary — and Chantal was a privileged friend of his. She forced herself to smile a smile that might have meant anything at all.

"I thought you already knew," she said.

He didn't press her. He stood for an instant, looking tall and forbidding, and then he relaxed and smiled at her.

"I'll keep an open mind," he said lightly. "Shall we go to the *medina?*"

They hurried down the broad Avenue, past the Cathedral towards the entrance of the old Arab town that hid behind thick, defensive walls as though it were still a hotbed of pirates that could expect angry retribution from across the sea.

It had been built long before cars had been thought of, with narrow winding passages that led one into the other, and all looked exactly the same, to the bewilderment of the stranger. First came the *souks,* streets of cell-like shops, gathered into their various trades, and selling everything from Woolworth ersatz to beautiful hand-made carpets from the holy city of Kairouan.

The passageways were thronged with people of every hue. Here and there a European would stand out against the flowing mass of Arabs, Moors and Berbers all around them. The women, full of eager talk and laughter, would stroll past them, modestly

26

veiling their faces with a corner of their *haik,* while their dark eyes gleamed with curiosity. The men, a trifle more self-assured, would stand and gossip, or bargain for hours as they did the shopping. It was always the men who would do the shopping, for the women were still mainly illiterate and couldn't count the money.

Katherine was glad of Dr. Kreistler's firm hand on her wrist. She was scared of getting lost in these long, bewildering passages that seemed to have no beginning and no end. The shopkeepers smiled at her and invited her in. There was no need to buy, they assured her. They would find chairs and she could sit and look at their wares in comfort. Perhaps she would like some coffee? Or some mint tea? When she passed them by, they would shrug their shoulders sadly, and she felt that they were genuinely sorry not to have had the chance of conversing with her.

The cobblers sat in the dark recesses of their shops, making the sandals that hung in clusters all round the entrance. The silversmiths on the other hand seemed to need more light and they would sit almost in the street, beating the silver with a tiny hammer, or picking out an intricate pattern with quick, confident hands. Mostly they made the typical Bedouin jewellery of enormous crescent moons and the ubiquitous Hand of Fatima that, with a bit of imagination, did look very like the hand of a woman.

Katherine picked one up and fingered it curiously. The filigree work on it, joining the fingers, was clumsy, but had a charm of its own. She put it down again with a faint feeling of regret.

"Bring you good luck, *mademoiselle!*" the silversmith told her, peering up at her over his work. "Keep away the evil eye!"

She shook her head. She had no need of charms, she didn't believe in them, but it was pretty and it was quaint, and she was beginning to think that she would need some kind of protection from Chantal's tongue. Resolutely she turned away from the shop and walked with quickened footsteps up the narrow alleyway. When people got to know her everything would be all right, she was sure of that. She had to be sure. And yet she couldn't say to everyone she met that she was a nurse and that she had hated having to give up her profession. And who would bother to ask her?

The husky whine of an Egyptian singer blared forth from half a dozen transistor sets, monotonous and yet strangely insistent to the ear, just as they were entering the Souk El Attarine. A Jewish cobbler on the corner sewed away on his treadle machine with a dreamy look on his face, his head bobbing up and down in time with the music. Katherine picked up two pins that had fallen down beside him and placed them carefully on the polished wood of his machine. He gave her a little nod of thanks, the smile just touching his eyes, though he was too shy to look at her for long.

Dr. Kreistler had no such scruples. He seemed to enjoy the sight of her expressive face as she looked about her.

"See a pin and pick it up, and all day you shall have good luck!" he teased her.

She blushed faintly, the pink rising slowly up her cheeks.

"How do you come to know English nursery sayings?" she asked him. "It sounds so strange coming from you!"

He was amused.

"I learned English at school," he said. His jaw tightened slightly. "English, French and Russian. We had a good teacher. I speak all three languages very well."

Katherine believed him. She wondered if he knew

that that was why she had picked up the pins. She gave him a quick glance through her eyelashes, but he was no longer looking at her. He was staring down at the far end of the *souks* where Chantal was standing, the light from one of the skylights picking her out like a spotlight.

"So she came after all!" the doctor muttered to himself. He turned, almost impatiently, to Katherine. "Come, we can catch her if we hurry!" he said.

He raced her down the passageway, scattering people to either side as they tried to get out of his way. A Bedouin woman, her face tattooed, and dressed in scarlet silk, scowled at him and shook her fist, but he called out something to her in Arabic and her frowns changed to laughter. Katherine hurried after him. She was frightened of losing him in the crowds and she was frightened of tripping on the rough ground.

Chantal stood and waited for them to catch up with her, an enigmatic little smile just playing on her lips.

"There was no hurry, *mon cher!*" she greeted the doctor, presenting one cool cheek for him to kiss. "I would have waited for you."

I'll bet! Katherine thought viciously. She wished that she didn't feel cheated, that she didn't resent the other girl's easy relationship with the doctor. What did he matter after all? He was only one person.

"And Kat-terine also!" Chantal went on, her eyes flickering up from Katherine's dusty shoes to her face that was hot with hurrying. "Guillaume was wondering what had happened to you. Could you not have told us if you meant to leave the hotel?"

Katherine found herself apologising, though she didn't see why she should. She wasn't answerable to these two for her actions!

"As it happened," the French girl added graciously, "I was able to tell him where you were, because it was I who asked Peter to show you round." She clung to his arm. "He makes a good guide, does he not?"

"Very good," Katherine agreed. She knew she sounded ungracious, but she couldn't help it. "We had just reached the beginning of the Souk El Attarine," she rushed on. "It looks very — very interesting."

Chantal's expression mocked her.

"Oh, it is!" she assured her. "Now that I am here we can all see it together." Her pale blue eyes rested on Dr. Kreistler's broad shoulders for an instant. "I need some more perfume," she complained softly. "It will be good for Katherine to see it being made, don't you think, Peter?"

"It is a pleasant sight," he agreed. His accent seemed to be more pronounced now that the other girl had arrived, and he looked faintly cross as though there were other things that he could think of to do with her — things that didn't include taking Katherine as well. "You could go together and start the proceedings," he suggested. "I have to go to the Kasbah to pick up some facts and figures for an article I am writing. I will return in a few minutes."

Chantal sighed.

"If you must!" she said tautly. "But I should have thought you could have forgotten about your work for one morning."

He smiled suddenly.

"You do your best to tempt me," he retorted. "And I might, if it were not Friday. But all the government offices close this afternoon for prayers and I must be getting back to Sidi Behn Ahmed."

"Of course," Chantal agreed coldly. "We shall be at the usual shop."

She walked away from him without a backward glance, her skirt swinging gently as she went. She certainly knew all that there was to know about dress, Katherine thought. And she wore her clothes with a confidence that made them seem even better than they were.

It was odd too, for the doctor looked faintly relieved as she went. For a man who had been so pleased to see her a few minutes earlier, he seemed quite as pleased to see her go.

Chantal stood at the entrance to one of the little shops and waited for Katherine to come up to her. She was still smiling that same enigmatic little smile.

"It will be a good thing for your happiness if you remember that Peter is mine," she said in quite friendly tones. "Absolutely mine!"

Katherine looked amused.

"So your brother told me last night," she said, and an unfortunate little devil crept up inside her. "I must say," she added, "I can't see Dr. Kreistler being *absolutely* anyone's! He seems to be dedicated to his work also."

Chantal treated that remark with the contempt that she obviously thought it deserved.

"A little hospital in the middle of nowhere? He will not be content with the Hospital of Fatima for very long, but a refugee must start somewhere and slowly gain people's confidence. One day we shall go to America and he will become a great man!"

"But surely —" Katherine began, and then stopped. It was none of her business. But she was sure that Guillaume had told her that Peter had been working for W.H.O. and had left to supervise the oasis hospital. If he had been as ambitious as Chantal made out, surely he would have done it the other way round? In that instant, and for the first time, she felt sorry for Chantal de Hallet.

The French girl was greeted as an old customer by the perfumier. He knew immediately which bottles to reach for and he started mixing the various ingredients together with all the care of a scientist.

It was a fascinating shop. Baskets full of henna powders, desiccated mint and verbena stood, spilling out, on the doorstep. Sticks of incense chips mixed with dried cloves gave a pungent spice to the atmosphere that was already full of the softer scent of rosepetals and beads fashioned out of ambergris and powdered Comoro-wood, with perhaps a dash of musk and one of true amber, the perfume fixed with civet. There was sandalwood too, apparently the favourite soap of the neighbourhood, and the array of brightly coloured bottles that were the extracts of a hundred different flowers; the gold of roses; the red of jasmine; the saffron yellow of verbena; and a dozen others.

Katherine looked at the prices on some of the jars and blinked. They may have been cheap by Paris standards, but they were still a great deal more than she had ever paid for a bottle of scent.

"I buy all my perfume here," Chantal told her. "Peter gave me the first lot and it has become a tradition now."

Katherine looked at the prices again. It hadn't occurred to her previously to wonder what Chantal did for money, but now she was frankly curious. Perhaps Guillaume made her an allowance from the money he received from the French estates, or perhaps her uncle had kept her? Katherine hoped not. It would make things even more awkward if she had to be tactful about that as well as everything else!

The perfumier measured out the last ingredient and held out the minute phial to Chantal.

"I can create something very special for your friend?" he suggested eagerly. "Something not too heavy —"

Katherine shook her head.

"I don't use a lot of perfume," she said.

Chantal made a face at her.

"No," she agreed. "I imagine surgical spirit would

32

be more in the line of the dedicated little nurse!"

Katherine bit her lip, determined not to show that the other girl's barbs were getting home. She was beginning to wonder how she could live in the same house as the de Hallets, and that would never do. She had to do it. She had to because Edouard de Hallet had expected it of her and he wouldn't have left her his properties for nothing.

"Aren't you going to pay for the perfume?" she asked quietly.

Chantal shrugged.

"Peter will pay when he comes," she said indifferently.

But for some reason Katherine was determined that that shouldn't happen. She opened her purse and handed over a note to the perfumier, receiving a few odd coins in exchange.

"Am I expected to thank you?" Chantal demanded.

"No," Katherine replied tautly. She couldn't explain her motives, they were too mixed up. But Peter Kreistler couldn't be a rich man. His salary would not be a very large one, working at a small hospital right down in the south of the country. And the perfume was so expensive. She didn't see why he should have to pay for it.

"It's a small present from me," she added pacifically.

Chantal looked first surprised and then amused.

"Then I suppose I ought to thank you," she said. "Or should I say: thank *you*, Uncle Edouard?"

Katherine looked her straight in the eyes.

"Whichever you please," she said calmly.

They stood in silence after that, one of them on either side of the doorway, waiting for Dr. Kreistler. It was so silly not to find something to talk about, and yet the more Katherine struggled to find a subject that was not labelled Dangerous, the less she could think of anything to say at all. It was with desperation that she finally managed:

"What are these baskets used for?" She pointed blindly at the satin-covered, padded baskets that hung in profusion over the doorway, and missed the fact that Dr. Kreistler had rejoined them until he said sharply, his accent more apparent than ever:

"Well, tell her, Chantal!"

The French girl opened her pale blue eyes very wide and smiled a secret smile.

"They are used at weddings," she said obligingly. "The bridegroom brings his presents for his bride in it."

"And afterwards they use it for the first-born child," the doctor supplied.

Katherine looked at one of the baskets more closely.

"They wouldn't last the child for long!" she said.

Dr. Kreistler looked at her with faint contempt.

"And how many babies have you had, Miss Lane?" he asked nastily.

Katherine chuckled.

"Me? Hundreds!" she said airily. It wasn't really a lie when she thought of all the babies that had come into the world under her care, but she found she couldn't quite meet Dr. Kreistler's eyes for all that. What a fool he would think her! And what a fool she was! Making conversation when she had always known that the Wise were Silent!

Dr. Kreistler had a Land Rover. The back seats and most of the floor space were piled high with the medical supplies he had come up to Tunis to collect. Chantal took one look and said she would take a taxi back to the hotel.

"You had better come with me," she said to Katherine, taking it for granted that the English girl would fall in with whatever plans she made. "Shall we see you at lunch, Peter?"

The doctor shook his head.

"I'll see you next time I come north." He kissed her lightly on the cheek and then turned to Katherine. "And you?"

Katherine took a deep breath to give herself courage.

"If I came to Sidi Behn Ahmed, could I help in the hospital?" she asked him urgently.

He bowed and kissed her hand, very much in the foreign manner.

"*If* you come I expect we could find you a job of some sort. But you won't come, Miss Lane. The Sahara is not for pretty-complexioned girls like you! Take my advice and stay at Hammamet." He turned abruptly and jumped up into the driving seat. "*Au revoir!*"

The two girls stood on the pavement and watched his car join the busy streams of traffic. Chantal sighed, and, to Katherine's dismay, two large tears rolled slowly down her cheeks.

"It is so sad to see him so seldom!" A fragile lacy handkerchief was brought out of her handbag, and with it the phial of perfume, that hit the pavement and splintered into a thousand pieces.

"Oh, look what I have done!" Chantal screamed.

Katherine stood by in silence, bitterly hurt. For an instant, so rapid that she might have imagined it, she had seen the look of triumph on the French girl's face as she had dropped the perfume.

To be hated that much was a frightening thing.

"Never mind," she heard herself saying automatically. "We can easily get some more."

Chantal wiped her eyes carefully on the edge of her handkerchief so as not to disturb her mascara.

"There is no time now!" she said with finality. "We leave straight after lunch."

She hailed a taxi and sat in the back seat, leaving it for Katherine to go round to the other side.

"By the way," she said silkily, "I forgot to tell you. I met some friends of ours this morning — Monsieur and Madame Verdon — and they wanted to travel home with us. I knew you wouldn't mind going in the estate car. It will be much easier for you really, not having to talk to us all the way."

Katherine said nothing. But at that moment she had never felt so alone in her whole life.

CHAPTER THREE

BECAUSE the hotel was not full, Katherine had been allowed to leave her suitcases in her room until after lunch. The bed had been stripped, however, and the shutters and window were as tightly closed as ever. She opened them, feeling a little guilty, but glad of the light breeze that played against the curtains, bringing the smell of distemper and sunshine into the room.

It was now, she thought, that she needed a solicitor. She needed some firm, *masculine* advice on what she should do. But, more than anything else, she needed someone to explain to her exactly what her position was, and more particularly, exactly what she ought to do about Chantal.

She didn't often smoke, but she smoked a cigarette now, very slowly, enjoying every moment of it. Then she washed her face and hands, re-did her hair, and went down to lunch.

Chantal made a very good hostess. She divided her time equally between her two guests, and if she was inclined to ignore Katherine's presence at the table, it wasn't made at all obvious. And Katherine had to admit that she liked her friends. Monsieur and Madame Verdon were a charming couple. They had lived in Tunisia since long before the war and had suffered with the local people when first the Germans and then the Allies had overrun their land. After the war they had rebuilt their farm and by dint of hard work and good judgment they were now both contented and very well off.

"We live not far from Hammamet," Madame Verdon told Katherine with a kind smile. "Chantal must bring you over to visit us."

Monsieur Verdon nodded his agreement.

"You have a very good man running your place," he told her thoughtfully, "but you might be glad of another opinion sometimes. You can always call on me." He smiled a trifle sadly. "Edouard was a friend of mine," he added quietly.

Katherine was terribly grateful to them both. She had always been accustomed to making friends quickly and easily, and these two seemed to be the first people in Tunisia who had been willing to like her at all.

She listened now eagerly as he told her all about the scheme Edouard de Hallet had had of introducing a small canning factory to cope with the excess of fruit that was grown.

"The idea was to have it on a co-operative basis, rather like the olive oil presses. There's quite a market for tinned fruit juice, and anyway it's much better than letting it rot round the trees as we have to do now whenever the market is glutted."

"Much better!" Katherine agreed. One did not have to be an expert to see that! "But why isn't the idea being carried out?"

Monsieur Verdon sighed.

"We needed Edouard's capital," he confessed. "The government were interested too, but with the vast expansion projects they have in hand they couldn't possibly help much. None of the rest of us has anything like the reserves needed."

"I see," Katherine said thoughtfully. Impulsively she touched him on the sleeve. "Perhaps we could still do it!" she exclaimed. "I don't really know what the estate consists of yet, but if the money was there before I presume it still is."

There was a sudden, uncomfortable silence all round the table.

"Edouard spent the money in his last year,"

Madame Verdon said at last. "And who could blame him? If ever a man loved life, it was he! He wanted to live more than anything else, and so it went, on doctors' bills and nursing homes, and things like that."

But it didn't! Katherine longed to protest. If he had said that, he must have been lying. He had spent some money, yes, but not all that. Didn't they know about the National Health Service in England? She allowed her eyelids to veil her eyes so that the others couldn't see what she was thinking. She had thought at the time that that was why he had gone to Britain at the end, because he couldn't afford the fantastic costs of being ill in a place like America, for instance. She had thought that he was an old, tired man who had been cast off by his family. A *rich* old man who had been too mean to spend his money on his own health and yet, on the other hand, wanting the very best of medical services. Silently, she apologised to him now. He must have had other reasons of his own for hiding the real way the money had gone, but that had been his own business and she could do nothing less than respect his wishes.

"Perhaps if we made economies it could still be done," she said hopefully.

It was Chantal who answered her. Her laugh, light and pretty, came floating across the table.

"And how should we live, my dear?" she asked. "Remember it is not only *you* that the estate supports!"

Katherine flushed, and was cross because she never had had any control over the rich, warm colour that flooded her cheeks at the slightest provocation. How could she ever forget? And she imagined that supporting Chantal was quite an expensive business.

"We can discuss it again when you have settled in at Hammamet," Monsieur Verdon said kindly. "We shall hope to see a great deal of you there."

Katherine flushed again, this time with happiness. She *liked* the Verdons immensely, and they seemed to like her too. If the other people at Hammamet were as nice, perhaps Chantal's attitude wouldn't matter so much. Perhaps she would even grow to like her!

She felt lonely again, though, when she stood on the steps of the hotel and watched the others get into Guillaume's car, ready to depart. The Verdons had been surprised that she was not to accompany them.

"There is plenty of room for three in the back," Madame had said.

Katherine had thrown Chantal a look of appeal that had been met by a stony stare.

"It — it isn't that," she had stammered. "It's just that I want to see the place on my own the first time. You know how it is."

Madame Verdon had plainly not known how it was, but she had accepted Katherine's explanation at its face value and had got into the back seat of the car.

They all waved as they left, except Chantal. She was far too busy investigating the corner of one of her nails. But Guillaume's bright blue eyes twinkled up at her reassuringly.

"The estate car is calling for you in a quarter of an hour," he told her above the roar of the traffic, and then, with one last wave, he pulled the car out into the middle of the avenue and they were gone.

Katherine went slowly back up the marble steps. Her suitcases were neatly piled beside the desk, and the receptionist smiled at her.

"Shall I ask the waiter to bring you some coffee in the *salon?*" he suggested to her. "I will let you know when the car comes."

Katherine thanked him. Now that that momentary depression had left her she could feel the excitement trembling inside her. There were difficulties to be faced and the challenge of somehow making a small canning plant possible. It was funny, but she felt more the trustee of Edouard Hallet's estate than its owner; even so, it was quite an adventure! She smiled happily to herself and sipped her coffee. She didn't care how long the car took to get there.

In actual fact it arrived sooner than it was expected and she had to down the last of her coffee in a hurry so as not to keep it waiting. It wasn't actually a car at all. It was more a miniature bus of the kind that they have on the Continent, that holds about six people and has a skylight in the roof that opens and windows all round the sides that don't.

The receptionist himself stowed her luggage away into the back, where it rubbed shoulders with a selection of mechanical spares and a couple of nylon net sacks of fresh vegetables.

"This is Beshir," he introduced the driver, and the two men greeted one another like long-lost friends, shaking hands and each slapping the other's back with playful hands.

Katherine got into the front seat, with Beshir beside her, chuckling away to himself at some joke the receptionist had made. He wore his *chechia,* his scarlet skull-cap, very far down over his eyes, and a pair of sunglasses that hid most of his face.

"It will be pleasant to have the company to Hammamet," he told her shyly, and then they settled themselves back in silence to enjoy the long drive.

It went surprisingly quickly. First there was the rather dull part as they went through the outskirts of Tunis itself with its phosphate factories and its other industries, but then they were out in the country, passing through the miles of vineyards (so odd to see in a Muslim country!) and the thousands and thousands of olive trees. It didn't look like Africa at all, it was far more like the other side of the Mediterranean, with its white-gashed hills and scrubby green vegetation. She knew she was in Africa, though, when she saw a camel being used to draw water from a well and another dragging a plough behind it between the olive trees.

Then at last they came to the orchards. The apricots and the peaches were already in bloom and the oranges hung large and heavy on their sweet-smelling branches just waiting to be picked. They were nearly there.

Beshir insisted on stopping at Nabeul for petrol. He grinned broadly at Katherine.

"You can have a cup of coffee — see the pottery. Best embroidery here in all Tunisia!"

Katherine agreed a trifle nervously and he left her standing on the pavement outside a café while he drove away in search of a garage. It was rather an alarming town, she thought, with black smoke belching over the housetops. She supposed they were firing the pottery, but what she could see of it, standing out on the pavements, she didn't like, and so she ordered herself a cup of coffee and sat out in the sunshine to drink it.

She wasn't alone for long. The children came and stared at her, smiling whenever they caught her eye and saying *"Bonsoir,"* as though it had some magic meaning which would keep them safe. Then as suddenly as they had come, they scattered away in all directions and only one man was left, tall and imperious, with his burnous gathered tightly around him.

"I am Brahim," he introduced himself. "I had not expected to meet you today or I should have been waiting for your arrival at Hammamet." He sat himself down with quiet dignity on a chair beside hers. "I am the manager of your estate," he explained.

Katherine hid her astonishment as best she could.

She held out her hand to him and liked the firm way he shook it. She looked at him with some embarrassment.

"I don't know the first thing about growing oranges and lemons," she burst out in a hurry, "so I do hope you will take me gently at first."

He smiled.

"It is not right to see a woman concerning herself with business," he said calmly. "I am an excellent manager. If I had not been, Monsieur de Hallet would not have employed me. The estate is doing well, for the land is rich and well tended, but it will not pay for all that the family demands from it." He finished speaking and sat in silence, waiting for her to add some comment. If it had not been for the cigarette he was smoking, he could have been sitting in the same place any time in the last two thousand years and not looked at all out of place.

"Have there been many demands?" Katherine asked at last.

He nodded gravely.

"Then they must stop," she said carefully. "Monsieur Verdon was telling me about the canning plant he and Monsieur de Hallet had planned to build. I — I promised him I'd try and find the money."

Brahim took a long puff from his cigarette.

"It is badly needed." He smiled with a sudden lightening of mood. "I shall bring the books in tonight for you to see and we can discuss it then, but I am afraid you will find it very difficult to manage. A lot of economies will have to be made."

It was Katherine's turn to laugh.

"I'm used to living on very little," she said. "What time will you come?"

He looked up at the sky and did some quick mental arithmetic.

"I shall come three hours after sunset."

"About nine o'clock?" Katherine confirmed in bewildered tones.

He nodded grandly.

"At that hour," he agreed. He stood up and held out his hand again. "The blessings of Allah be with you, Miss Lane."

She swallowed.

"And with you!" she replied faintly.

Her coffee seemed rather dull and ordinary after that. She thought she would need at least a hubble-bubble pipe to live up to Brahim, and the idea amused her. But then the smile on her face sobered into a frown. It was all very well to make economies, but would anyone pay the faintest attention to her dictates? She sighed. There was no doubt about it, telling the de Hallets that they were not going to get as much money in future was not going to be easy.

Beshir was full of the lucky coincidence of Brahim being in Nabeul at just that particular moment when he brought back the car. For the first time Katherine saw that there was some resemblance between them, and she asked if they were related.

"We are brothers," Beshir agreed. He took off his dark glasses and she saw that they really were very alike indeed, despite the fact that one of them wore Western dress and the other the costume traditional to the desert.

"Brahim will see you tonight? He has been worried all week by the bills that have come in. There has been no living with him!" the younger brother grinned.

"What bills?" Katherine demanded.

He shrugged his shoulders.

"Hotel bills; bills for clothes; all kinds of bills!"

De Hallet bills! Oh well, they would have to be paid. There was no good getting upset about it, especially not before she had even seen them, but somehow that canning factory seemed suddenly very far away indeed.

It was only a short drive between Nabeul and Hammamet. It seemed only a few seconds between leaving one small town and entering the other, with the same flat distempered houses with blue painted windows and doors and the same narrow streets into which only an occasional door opened. The Arabs hugged their privacy and built their houses looking inwards over a central square, and there was really very little to see from the outside.

Katherine thought she had never seen such a lovely place as Hammamet. Orchards clustered round the small town, and beyond was the sea as blue as she had ever seen it. Wild flowers grew in profusion everywhere and the odd glimpses she had inside some of the pleasure gardens made her gasp as she saw the vivid splashes of colour that filled all the beds.

But it was her own house that reduced her to silence. The elaborate wrought-iron gates should have prepared her, but did not. The long drive was lined with trees and was pleasantly cool, and ended in a wide square in which a fountain played. But it was the house behind the square that commanded all one's attention. It was large and Moorish in character, with wide verandahs and arches everywhere. Bougainvillea hung over the doorways, vivid purple splashes, so heavily in bloom that they had to be supported with long wooden stakes.

Katherine got out of the car and stood in the middle of the square, just looking about her. She had never seen anything like it — and to imagine that it all belonged to her!

Beshir blew the horn with gusto and deposited her suitcases on the nearest verandah.

"Someone come soon and show you inside," he told her cheerfully, and was gone in a cloud of dust back down the drive.

Someone did come. A Negro came running out of the front door, dressed in highly embroidered camel-trousers and a Spanish type coat. He came to a full stop when he saw Katherine, and beamed with pleasure.

"Madame? I thought perhaps it was Madame de Hallet. Madame has business here?"

Katherine pointed to her suitcases.

"I am Miss Lane," she said with a smile.

Eagerly he seized the cases and led the way into the house. It was just as lovely inside. Thick local carpets covered the floors and embroidered blankets from the island of Djerba hung on the walls like tapestries. But it was the vistas of arches, one leading into another for as far as the eye could see, that was the loveliest feature. There was no overburdening the rooms with furniture either. A few pieces, old and polished to a fine gloss, stood here and there, expensive and lovely.

A little awed, Katherine allowed herself to be led to her bedroom and was glad to see that she had a perfectly normal bed, even if it were covered with another embroidered blanket to give it a touch of the exotic.

"Madame is hot?" the Negro asked her anxiously as she threw open the shutters. "Shall I bring a pressed lemon with ice?"

Katherine grinned. A *pressed* lemon! With lemons from her very own trees! The Negro grinned too, aware of an overpowering sense of relief. It had been whispered in the market place that Mademoiselle Lane would not come, that Mademoiselle de Hallet would take over the estate. But she had come and she had eyes that he could see, not pale like that other one's, and she was nice.

"I bring it straight away," he said.

Guillaume had brought a bottle of the very best

wine that the country produced as a peace-offering for Katherine.

"I felt so badly about leaving you to come on alone," he told her. "Will this make up for it?" His bright blue eyes looked straight into hers and she could feel her defences against him melting.

"Don't be silly!" she said sharply. "I didn't mind a bit."

He held the wine over her head, just out of her reach.

"Little liar!" he teased her. "Admit it and the bottle's yours!"

She laughed.

"All right, I admit it!" She accepted the bottle from him and put it in the middle of the table. "And how about your admitting that it was just as much your idea as it was Chantal's?"

His blue eyes clouded over.

"But it wasn't, Kathy! Truly it wasn't. I wouldn't have had it happen for anything, but once she gets the bit between the teeth — Well, you know how it is!"

"Yes, I know how it is," Katherine said grimly. "And *don't* call me Kathy!"

"No, ma'am!"

They smiled at one another with a new understanding. Guillaume could be very charming, Katherine thought, and he would help her if he could, but he was no match for that sister of his, and he knew it. She would have to stand on her own two sturdy feet and like it. And it was no good thinking of Dr. Peter Kreistler either, she told herself angrily, for he was already in the other camp!

They were still standing by the table when Chantal made her entrance. She had changed for dinner, and for the first time Katherine thought she had lost that touch of chic. Tonight she was frankly over-dressed.

47

Her pale eyes flickered over them both as she moved towards the chair at the head of the table.

"I hear that you've already met Brahim," she said to Katherine. "I hope you didn't pay any attention to his pessimistic mumblings. Uncle Edouard and I always used to call him the Prophet — he's forever prophesying doom and disaster for someone!"

Guillaume laughed.

"He certainly looks the part!" he said.

Katherine didn't say anything.

"Well?" Chantal demanded.

Katherine held her head up high and looked the other girl straight in the face.

"He's bringing the books for me to see tonight," she said clearly. "And he did mention a few bills that would have to be paid."

Guillaume groaned. "My car, I expect!" he said philosophically.

Katherine was shocked. "Your car?" she repeated.

He shrugged his shoulders in an expressive French gesture.

"You don't suppose I manage on what I get from France, do you?"

Chantal sat down with a slight, malicious grin on her face. She nodded to the servant to bring in the food and spread her napkin carefully over her knees. That was another thing that would have to change, Katherine thought. *She* was the hostess now, not Chantal, and the sooner she made that clear the easier it would be for everyone. But not tonight, she excused herself wearily. She was too tired tonight to start another battle.

"How much do you take from the Tunisian estates?" she asked Guillaume.

Chantal's eyes sparkled.

"Yes, tell us, Guillaume," she bade him. "Is it one hundred or two hundred a month? Katherine is bound to want to know! She's the kind to count every penny, no matter how big the pile."

Katherine blenched. One or two *hundred!* What on earth did he spend it on?

"It seems an awful lot," she said out loud.

Guillaume gave her a pitying look.

"That's nothing! You should ask Chantal what she manages to get through!"

Chantal, it seemed, was only too willing to tell her. She laughed down in her throat, as though she was glad to know that the figure would be more money than Katherine had seen in a lifetime.

"Uncle Edouard gave me a basic allowance of two-fifty a month," she began sweetly. "But of course I couldn't possibly manage on so little. I sent all the other little bills to him."

"I see," Katherine said coldly. "Well, I'm afraid you're going to have to manage on a great deal less. I can't believe the estate alone produces anything like that amount —"

"Why not?" they both demanded in unison. "It always has!"

Katherine quietly finished her soup.

"Has it?" she asked them. "Or did your uncle pay the bills out of capital?"

Guillaume flushed.

"That was just a yarn of his," he said. "Nobody *likes* shelling out, you know." But he looked a bit subdued all the same. "What are you going to do?" he asked at length.

"I shall give you each a fixed allowance from the proceeds of the estate," she said. There was a slight quiver in her voice, and she wished it would go away because she couldn't afford to have them argue with her. "Any bills you run up over and above that, you'll have to pay yourselves," she ended on a firmer note.

"And I suppose you'll grab the rest!" Chantal put in spitefully.

49

Katherine bit her lip. What was she going to do? It seemed so silly of her not to have given her own financial position a thought. She had a certain amount of money that she had managed to save and she knew she could have two hundred and fifty pounds of it sent out to her from England. If she went carefully she ought to be able to manage on that. It wasn't as if she would be having to pay any rent or taxes or anything like that.

"I shan't take a penny," she announced proudly. "Anything that's left over will go towards the canning factory."

Chantal gave her a look of complete disbelief and Guillaume one of dawning respect.

"Good for you," he said in shaky tones. "But how will you live?"

The room seemed lighter somehow, as though somebody had switched on the lights, although she knew they hadn't. She felt lighter and she was beginning to enjoy herself. She looked round the magnificent room and felt free of it. Through the arch she could see the drawing-room, with the copper-topped tables and the comfortable chairs. It was all like a dream and the extraordinary thing was that, amidst all this splendour, she was glad to be waking up. She wouldn't stay in Hammamet at all, she decided. There was nothing for her to do there. Brahim would run the estate and Chantal would run the house no matter how often or how much she objected.

It had always been the same, she remembered, whenever she had made a big decision. There had been that day when she had been asked if she would like the Casualty Ward of the hospital where she had trained. It had been a tremendous compliment to her professional abilities, she had known that. And yet she had finally turned it down to go into private nursing because she had wanted more contact with the people she had nursed. That had been her one fault as a nurse, she thought, she had always had the tendency to become too involved in the lives and troubles of her patients.

She took a deep breath and put up a hand to push in an errant pin in her hair.

"I shall go down and help in the hospital at Sidi Behn Ahmed," she said. "I shan't need a great deal of money down there."

"You mean *work* in the hospital?" Guillaume asked. "Peter would never allow you to!"

But Chantal knew better.

"Oh yes, he'll allow you to work!" she said venomously. "He'll allow you to work yourself to death, and he won't even notice you're there! So don't expect any gratitude for your noble gesture, will you, Nurse Katherine Lane?"

CHAPTER FOUR

KATHERINE sent a message by telephone to the Hospital of Fatima telling them that she would be arriving within the next day or so, and then went to her room to pack. It was late, for the session with the books had taken longer than she had intended. Brahim had brought them punctually at nine, but it had been well after midnight before they had finished calculating the finances of the estate and deciding how much could be allocated to the various demands that were made on it.

She and Brahim had drunk tea in the way of the Sahara, with the first cup weak, the second strong and very sweet and the third equally strong but bitter, and they had reluctantly set apart the greater amount of the profits for the benefit of the de Hallets.

Afterwards Katherine had walked in the spacious pleasure gardens. It had been another night like the first one she had known in Tunisia, with the stars so close that one could almost pick them out of the sky and with the trees making strange shapes against the silver of the moon. To her surprise Guillaume had come out to join her. She hadn't been able to see the vivid blue of his eyes in the darkness, she had only seen the weakness of his chin and mouth and the rather endearing way he had of waiting for approval like an over-anxious puppy.

"I suppose you think we are a couple of worms," he had opened the conversation.

She had smiled in the darkness.

"No, why should I?" she had replied gently.

He hadn't said anything for a moment, then suddenly he had said,

"I am glad you're going from here. Chantal would

hurt you if she could, and you're too nice for that."
He had smiled and she had seen the whiteness of
his teeth in the moonlight. "And don't let that doctor
overwork you either! He and Chantal are two of a
kind. I should know," he added gloomily, "I've
known one of them all my life and the other ever
since he arrived here in 1956."

"Wh-what do you mean?" she had asked, her
voice suddenly husky.

He had looked surprised.

"I should have thought it was obvious. They're
both completely single-minded when it comes to getting their own way. People to them are pawns to be
moved round the board."

Katherine sighed, going to the window of her room
and gazing out at the scene beyond. In the far distance she could just see the black line that was the
sea and the palm-trees that edged the beach. Nearer
to her was one of the smaller orchards and the rock
garden, surrounded by moonflowers that gleamed
white and romantic in the moonlight.

Dr. Peter Kreistler was as good as engaged to
Chantal. It would be as well to remember that. She
pulled herself up abruptly. She wasn't going down
to Sidi Behn Ahmed to see Dr. Kreistler. She was
going down to work! She had worked with all kinds
of doctors before and none of them had ever worried her. It would be ridiculous if she allowed herself
to get all het up about this one. Ridiculous and silly
and unprofessional, and she had no intention of being
any of those things.

She undressed rapidly and got into bed. The soft
light of the night showed up the Moorish arch of
the window and the intricate metalwork that covered
it to keep out intruders. It was foreign and entranc-
ingly different. It was funny, she thought, that she
should be glad to be leaving this place. And yet she

was glad. She would be glad to be back with her own work, glad to be useful once again.

When she awoke, her early morning tea had already been brought to her, and with it a buff-coloured envelope. She sat up and looked at it for a long time before she opened it. It had *Télégramme* written in large black letters on one corner and, presumably, the same word in Arabic on the other. Who on earth would be sending her a telegram here, in Tunisia?

The paper of the envelope was cheap and tore like blotting paper when she opened it. With fumbling fingers she drew out the sheet inside and stared down at it.

STAY EXACTLY WHERE YOU ARE UNTIL FURTHER NOTICE. KREISTLER.

She read it through twice and she could feel the prickle of her temper on the back of her neck. How dared he? she demanded of herself. How dared he dictate to her like that? Perhaps Guillaume had been right. Perhaps people were no more to him than pawns to be moved round a board. Well, she was moving to Sidi Behn Ahmed, whether he liked it or not, and she was going today!

But it wasn't quite as easy as she had imagined. The distances involved were so much greater than she was accustomed to, and even if the roads were good, she didn't see how they could possibly get there in one day.

Beshir, however, had no qualms about anything. "Today we shall go as far as Kairouan," he announced. "Very fine city, as you shall see. Then long day tomorrow to Sidi Behn Ahmed."

She looked at where he was pointing on the map and agreed with him. She didn't want him to know that her heart failed her when she saw the vast empty spaces of the south. There were fewer and fewer green splashes on the map down there — nothing but large areas of white occasionally interrupted by the blue dots that marked the most important of the salt lakes.

"Is it really safe for a small car to go off like that, by itself?" she asked Chantal after breakfast.

The French girl shrugged her shoulders.

"Are you now afraid to go?" she demanded.

Was that it? It might be true, but it wasn't so much the land she was afraid of as the circumstances. The map didn't show the garages, and what if they were to get a series of punctures miles from anywhere?

"I wondered if the tank would hold sufficient petrol," she murmured.

Chantal shrugged again.

"It is usual to take extra in tins," she said.

Katherine began to think she was worrying needlessly when Beshir brought round the car and she found that he had already filled a couple of five-gallon tins and had them strapped on securely to the back of the mini-bus. There were a couple of spare tyres too and some long rolls of canvas for use in case they ran into some loose sand drifting across the road.

"All is ready!" Beshir called to her triumphantly. He seemed pleased to think that he was going to be at the wheel for two solid days.

Katherine waited for her luggage to be put in the back and then climbed into the front seat herself. Surprisingly, both the de Hallets had come out to see her off, Chantal looking withdrawn and very glad to see the back of her, and Guillaume a little guilty.

Beshir opened the skylight behind and roared the engine until he got exactly the sweet note of response he wanted.

"Right, we go!" he shouted, and sounded the klaxon hooter with enthusiasm. A number of children who had been standing eyeing them from a distance crept a little closer and smiled shyly at the scene.

Chantal put a hand on either side of the open car door and put her head right inside the cabin. For a moment Katherine thought she was going to give her a kiss of farewell, and her heart gave a little lurch within her, but the blatant dislike in Chantal's eyes was as apparent as ever.

"Goodbye, *mon amie*," she whispered. "And remember, for your own good, Peter belongs to me!"

As if she was likely to forget it!

"You can give him a message from me," the French girl went on, her eyes glinting with sudden, suppressed laughter. "Tell him that the medicine he prescribed worked only too well and that I should like some more of the same next time he comes!"

Katherine averted her eyes from that beautifully made-up, sleek face, and nodded. She could very well imagine what the medicine had been and she was annoyed to discover that the thought didn't please her. Of course it was only because Chantal was so blatantly unsuited to being a doctor's wife, but even so it was ridiculous to allow herself to get upset. Many other doctors had married apparently unsuitable wives and had managed very well. She must be getting narrow-minded, allowing her own prejudices to affect her judgment.

"I'll tell him," she agreed bleakly.

The French girl stepped back from the car and they started forward down the drive, a soft cloud of dust blowing out behind them. Guillaume waved and Katherine waved back to him, suddenly sorry to be leaving him behind. He was at least someone she knew — and liked! For she did like him. He was spoilt and weak, but there was no harm in him. She shivered slightly. He was certainly not dangerous in the same way as his sister was. Chantal left a decidedly bad taste in the mouth, with her menacing threats and her dislike that sometimes veered over the border into hatred. It was nice to think that she was leaving her behind as well.

Beshir drove very fast, in the French manner, with a showy pride in his skill and a delight in the klaxon horn that he occasionally varied by the softer horn that the makers had provided. Katherine found the long straight roads hypnotic. Rows and rows of olive trees stretched to either side for as far as she could see, each tree in its own saucer of earth, specially designed for the most economical use of the water. The ground was all beautifully ploughed and neatly kept, and sometimes vegetables had been planted in the shade provided by the trees.

"I suppose the oil is very valuable?" Katherine asked Beshir.

He laughed.

"I should say! In the Sahel district each tree will bear between two and three hundred pounds of fruit."

Katherine looked at the trees with new interest, imagining them as they would be later, laden with olives.

"How much oil does that make?"

Beshir waved his hands expansively over the steering-wheel.

"In a good year, when the rains are good, one needs perhaps ten pounds to make a kilo. In not such a good year, perhaps fifteen." He looked about him with satisfaction. "Soon, when the government plans are complete, we shall have as many olive trees in Tunisia as there were in the Roman times. Everywhere you will see more trees being planted!"

She did too. At Enfidaville they passed through the government-sponsored estates and she was impressed by the hard work that had been put into the ground everywhere. Even the poorer steppe lands were being reclaimed and villages of brand new little box-shaped houses clustered round the sources of water, providing new homes for the nomadic tribes of Bedouin that wandered through the land. Sometimes she saw a cluster of the waist-high black tents, guarded by a couple of haughty camels and one hobbled donkey, and the Bedouin children would rush out to see the car pass by.

The land grew poorer still and there were only the tough clumps of esparto grass and the hedges of prickly pear to show that anyone lived there at all. And then, quite suddenly, Kairouan was there, her white domes and minarets towering above her walls. The city the Aghlabite dynasty had built to impress the stubborn Berber people into accepting their Muslim religion rose out of the flat miles of dust in splendid beauty, like some dream of the Arabian nights. Katherine leant forward in her seat and gasped.

"Is this Kairouan?" she asked unbelievingly. She thought of the dry salt lakes and the damp muddy flats they had just come through and wondered how anyone could possibly have conceived of building a city in such a place.

Even Beshir was silent for a minute.

"Yes," he said at last, "this is Kairouan."

They drove through the narrow, dust-covered streets at the usual reckless pace, scattering pedestrians all around them as they leaped for safety, their brown faces breaking into ready laughter as the mini-bus tore past them.

The flags were out, splashes of scarlet against the white walls and the dark, blue-black shadows. Beshir stopped the car and called out something to a tall man with a bright pink towel wrapped round his head like a turban. The man pointed up another street and Beshir reversed and went up it, coming to a full stop outside a small hotel.

Opposite were some gardens, with green grass and flowers and a statue of President Bourguiba. It was a small oasis of cool colour in the glare of white walls that reflected the rays of the hot sun above. Katherine got out of the car and went over to it, peering through the surrounding iron bars. It reminded her of England and, not for the first time, she wondered why she had ever accepted Edouard de Hallet's legacy.

Beshir opened up the back of the mini-bus and pulled her luggage out on to the pavement. The bags were covered with a film of white dust and, looking at it, Katherine thought that she too must be in very much the same way. If her hair had been shorter she could have washed it, but as it was it would have to wait until she reached Sidi Behn Ahmed. She made a little gesture of distaste, disliking her grimy appearance, and entered the hotel with resolution. A good, cool wash would be a help anyway, and a complete change of clothes.

The entrance to the hotel was just like walking into an oriental bazaar. Piles of carpets covered the flooring and curtains of beads hung in gay profusion across all the doors. One or two uncomfortable carved chairs stood round the walls, separated by copper trays that served as tables. Only the narrow vista of the bar that led out of the hallway spoilt the exotic impression. It was as dimly lit as any American equivalent and full of Europeans.

Katherine stood for an impatient moment, waiting for the receptionist to notice her. When at last he looked up, she opened her mouth to speak, but the words died before she ever uttered them. He looked straight beyond her, over her shoulder, and she found herself turning to look also. And there, in the doorway of the bar, looking like a thundercloud, was Dr. Kreistler.

He stood there for a long moment, and although she was accustomed to irate Sisters — indeed, she had been one herself when her own superior had been away — she had to admit that none of them had ever made her feel so uncomfortable as he was doing now. One hand crept up to her collar and she wished earnestly that she had at least had time to change.

"Well, Miss Lane?" he said at last.

She tried to pull herself together. What was it to him what she did?

"Dr. Kreistler!" she breathed, and promptly wished she had said nothing at all. She had sounded so surprised and so very unsure of herself.

"In person," he agreed silkily. He crossed the room towards her, his shoes completely silent on the thick carpets. He looked taller and capable of almost anything at all, and it was only with the greatest difficulty that she stopped herself from shrinking away from him against the reception desk. "I thought my telegram was quite explicit," he went on.

She recollected his telegram with a wave of anger.

"Explicit!" she stormed at him. "It was quite clear as to meaning, if that's what you mean!'

His eyes glinted dangerously.

"I am glad to hear it," he said softly, and she was suddenly afraid again.

"You had no right—" she began. She stopped, coming face to face with the blank wall of his disapproval. "I—I won't be shouted at!" she said instead, and was horrified to hear the dinstinctly sulky note that had entered her voice.

"I have no intention of shouting at you," he replied. "I don't shout at people. But I agree that this is not the place to continue this discussion. We'll go and take a walk in the gardens." His hand closed round her wrist in a purposeful manner and perforce she had to follow him out again into the sunshine.

He let her go at the foot of the statue and she rubbed her wrist resentfully, hating him.

"Have I hurt you?" he demanded.

"No," she admitted, incurably truthful. "But—"

To her surprise her grinned.

"But you couldn't resist making the most of it!" he supplied for her. "You're really very feminine, aren't you, Miss Lane?"

She didn't know quite how to answer that so she looked down at her shoes instead and saw that they too were looking travel-stained and badly in need of a clean. When she looked up again the faint gleam of humour had gone.

"I am an extremely busy man," he said coldly. "At the moment I am running six local clinics apart from the central hospital at Sidi Behn Ahmed. I haven't got the time to go chasing round the country after errant females who have more money than sense!"

Katherine's eyes opened wide. Well, that was the first time anybody had ever accused her of that!

"Nobody asked you to go chasing round the country, Dr. Kreistler," she said with dignity.

He sighed.

"You are not now living in England," he told her patiently. "This is a Muslim country where women do not travel alone without escorts."

"I had Beshir," she objected doggedly.

"Beshir! Beshir!" he repeated scornfully. "Why on earth couldn't you have done what you were told? I should have come north for you as soon as possible, if that was what you really wanted to do. As it is I have had to leave a nurse in charge of the hospital because no other arrangements could be made at such short notice, and I am not in the habit of having to neglect my patients for *anyone at all*!"

That she could well believe.

"I'm sorry," she said, feeling a little stupid.

Surprisingly, this seemed to anger him still more.

"Sorrow is a very easy emotion!" he snorted. "It

will be on your head if anything happens while I am away."

Katherine leaned againnst the statue. She was hot and tired and she was becoming aware that the dust that had got into everything else was also choking up her throat in the most uncomfortable way.

"How did you know," she asked in flat tones, "that I had come to Kairouan?"

He looked away from her, far across the gardens.

"I rang them up at Hammamet and they told me," he answered. "They seemed rather upset that you should choose to leave them so rapidly," he added dryly.

Oh, were they! To her dismay a tear trickled down her cheek, and when she brushed it impatiently away she knew that the mark of it could be clearly seen against the dust on her cheeks. She turned to him with anxiety in her eyes.

"You will allow me to work at the hospital, won't you?" she insisted. "I told them that that was what I was going to do."

He shrugged his shoulders.

"I expect we can find you something," he agreed reluctantly. "But there is no room for the amateur when it comes to a person's health. You are not to mess around with things you don't understand, is that clear?"

She wanted to tell him then that she was a nurse. Why hadn't the de Hallets told him that? she wondered. And why couldn't she tell him now? But she couldn't. His attention had turned away from her and back to the hotel.

"I have booked you a room," he told her. "I suggest you go and have a quick shower and then I'll arrange for you to have something to eat."

She nodded her head. She hadn't realised that she was hungry, but now that he suggested food the mere thought of it made her feel faint.

"Have you — have you also booked a room for Beshir?" she asked him bravely.

He looked at her in surprise, as though he hadn't expected her to be concerned about her chauffeur.

"I have," he said quietly, and he gave her a gentle push in the back. "Go quickly," he bade her. "You look like a lost child, without any make-up and with dust on your eyelashes." He smiled in that sudden way he had. "A nice child," he added with a laugh. "A job will be good for you. A little discipline is all you need to make you into quite a nice person!"

And such was the chaos of her thoughts that her normally only too ready tongue couldn't find a single word to answer him. Instead she fled across the garden, over the street, and into the hotel, without a single backward glance.

She felt better when she had washed and changed, and with her heart doing peculiar things at the thought of going downstairs to face him again, she made up her face with a lavish hand, eye-shadow, mascara — the lot! It made her feel very grown-up and sophisticated, but when she had finished she found she didn't like it very much and took it all off again. Angrily she faced her reflection in the looking glass.

"So you look like a child, do you?" she addressed it crossly, and had to admit that, with her hair hanging in two plaits down her back, she didn't look much older than a schoolgirl.

The second time she was more careful when she applied the eye-shadow and she was pleased with the result. It attracted attention to the luminous quality of her eyes, and she was pleased to notice that they were really a much better shape than were Chantal's. With the ease born of long practice she switched her hair up into position and fastened it with a few pins. It gave her confidence to see her hair in its normal, staid style, and she smiled at herself. She certainly didn't look a child now!

But if he noticed all the trouble she had taken he didn't give any sign of it. He made her sit down at a table in one corner of the dining-room and stood over her while she ate the *casse-croûte* he had ordered for her — an enormous torpedo sandwich, filled with tunny fish and pickles moistened with olive oil. He had ordered coffee for two, she noticed with relief, as she struggled through the enormous bread roll. At least she wouldn't have to drink all that by herself also.

"Will that hold you until dinner time?" he asked her as she swallowed the last mouthful.

"It's more likely to have sunk me by then!" she retorted.

He laughed with a singular lack of feeling for her sensibilities.

"It is foolish to go without one's meals!" he told her sharply.

"Yes, Dr. Kreistler," she agreed meekly.

He made an impatient noise and got restlessly to his feet. Didn't the man ever relax? With his hands in his pockets he stared moodily out of the window, before turning to face her again.

"Come," he said. "Let us go out and walk around the streets. Hotels are boring places to be in, do you not agree?"

She was too startled to answer. Boring? No she had never thought of them as being *that!* She collected her handbag and smiled at him.

"Come on, then," she agreed. "I'm ready."

He led her rapidly through the narrow streets, stopping every now and then to point something out to her. Once it was the blue painted ironwork over a harem window; once it was young dried eucalyptus leaves that had been impregnated with D.D.T. and hung on a wall to keep the flies away; and once to point out the school where the young girls learned to make their famous carpets.

"Do you want to see inside?" he asked.

Katherine nodded.

She was surprised by the cool, clean buildings, where the giant looms stood in rows, tended by the little girls. In the morning, he told her, they now went to school, as their mothers had never done, but in the afternoons they learned the intricacies of their ancient trade, so that when they had passed their diplomas and married they could set up on their own and contribute towards the family wage.

He took her to see the famous mosques also — the Mosque of the Barber, where the friend of Mahomet is buried with three hairs of the Prophet's beard, and the Grand Mosque, the Mosque of Sidi El Akbar, with its stolen Roman columns and enormous square. With casual hands he removed his shoes and stood by expectantly while she did the same, before taking her into the enormous prayer room.

"This is the only mosque I know where an infidel can do this," he said with satisfaction, and wandered over to look at the elaborately carved Imam's chair, completely forgetting all about her.

Katherine wandered round too, fascinated by the mats that were tied round the base of each column, carefully padding their hard edges against over-enthusiastic worshippers. But more than anything else she watched Dr. Kreistler padding over the rush mats, as pleased as any small child allowed to take off his shoes and spread his toes on something strange for a change.

She was footsore and weary when they got back to the hotel. It wasn't that Dr. Kreistler had walked her so very far, but he had walked her so *fast!* And she should never have worn her best shoes, their heels were far too high for sight-seeing, as any fool could have told her!

It was only half-past nine when she went to her room for the night. She pushed back the shutters and found she could see straight into the courtyard of a house opposite. Two little girls were playing ball against a wall, one of them with her veil slung round her shoulders, the other in jeans, her discarded veil flung on to the ground. Katherine smiled to herself. The American influence had even reached the harem, she thought, and was glad.

Idly she yawned and pulled the curtains, shutting out the little scene. She was glad that she too was feminine and found herself blushing. Well, Dr. Kreistler had thought so anyway, hadn't he? She eased her shoes off her aching feet and knocked the two heels together, tapping out a tune of her own making to herself. She had got to know Dr. Kreistler quite well that evening, she thought, and all that she knew of him she liked. He was *nice!* Really nice! And she was glad she was to have his company during the long drive south the next day.

She felt again his fingers as they had brushed her face when he had said goodnight to her, dismissing her as though she really was no more than a child. She had liked the way he had done it though, and tomorrow — She froze. Whatever was she thinking of? A few kind words and her wits were scattered in the silliest, most *feminine* way! Dr. Peter Kriestler had Chantal to say goodnight to, and he probably did it very thoroughly too when he was staying up north, at Hammamet! He wouldn't just flick·*her* cheek with his fingers! And he certainly wouldn't refer to her as a nice child in need of discipline.

With a little sob, she pulled off her clothes and dropped them on the floor, jumping into bed and pulling the bedclothes right up over her head.

CHAPTER FIVE

KATHERINE awoke to hear someone pounding on her door.

"Oui," she called out sleepily. *"Entrez!"* But whoever it was had already gone. She glanced at her watch and saw that it was just six o'clock. The first stirrings of the day could be heard out in the streets and she could hear the faithful being called to prayer, in the modern way, over a faulty microphone that sounded out across the city. It was, she supposed, time to get up.

It took her only a few minutes to wash and dress and pack the few things she had needed for the night, and then she hurried downstairs to breakfast. Dr. Kreistler was already there, impatiently glancing at his watch as though he were already in a hurry to be gone. Katherine took her seat beside him, hiding a smile of amusement. Really, he had the energy of three men, and expected everyone else to be the same. He probably *did* the work of three men too, and thought it quite normal. She wondered where he had trained and what he had specialised in, but didn't like to ask him. She was already beginning to think of his work as a dangerous topic, and she had absolutely no intention of quarrelling with him today!

When the coffee came it was hot and good and the rolls that went with it were crisp and still warm from the oven. Katherine ate her share in silence, aware at times of his eyes on her but not knowing what to say. One way and another she was glad when the meal was over and she could disappear to get her luggage down from her room.

When she got down to the hallway again, Beshir had already driven off and there was only the doctor's Land Rover standing in front of the hotel, the dark green khaki covered with a thick layer of dust that had collected into patterns on the canvas seats and roofing. Katherine brushed it off as well as she could, but it was a hopeless task, the dust settling again as fast as she could remove it.

Dr. Kreistler watched her in silence for one long, impatient moment.

"Oh, get in!" he said at last. "A little dust won't hurt you. It will be worse once we leave the good roads."

Chagrined, she bit her lip, and stepped up into the Land Rover, sitting down quickly on the hard, unsprung seat.

"I would much rather have travelled in the minibus," she complained. "At least in it one had some protection against all this!" She waved her hand round, pointing at the piles of dust that had collected in every corner.

Dr. Kreistler chuckled.

"I don't suppose you're nearly as fragile as you suppose!" he retorted. "And I like to have you under my eye where I can see what you're up to!"

Just as though she was, in very truth, a child! She stowed her handbag away on the central seat and crossly surveyed the scene in front of her.

"And *don't* drink the water anywhere south of here!" he added crushingly. "I don't want you down with dysentry as well as everything else."

"I'm not a complete fool, Dr. Kreistler," she said primly. "I shouldn't dream of drinking *any* water unless I knew where it had come from."

He sprang up beside her and she was suddenly very glad of the empty seat between them. It gave her a sense of distance that she was beginning to appreciate.

"Is that so?" he drawled. "Well, see that you stick to your good intentions, Miss Lane!"

She had not realised before how *intensely* she disliked being addressed by her surname — especially by Dr. Kreistler! He made it sound as though it had two syllables, ending it with an insufferable finality that irritated her more than she could say. She glowered at him, but he didn't even notice. He merely shoved the gear lever into the right position, depressed the clutch, and drove, as though the gates of hell had opened up behind him, straight out of the city.

Katherine found it safer to hook one hand round the edge of her seat and to hang on. She was terrified of being thrown right out of her perilous perch and there seemed to be nothing between her and the road that flashed past beside her. But she soon discovered that Dr. Kreistler might drive fast but he also drove well, with a fierce concentration that somehow enabled him to avoid all the worst of the ruts and the bumps in the road.

"Which way are we going?" she asked after she had suffered in silence for as long as she could bear.

"Via Sbeitla. There's a map in the pocket just in front of you if you want to have a look."

The idea of her coping with a map as well as everything else struck her as funny, and a little gasp of laughter escaped from her. He gave her a suspicious look and slowed down considerably.

"I'm sorry," he apologised. "I am apt to forget that most people find it necessary to become acclimatised to my driving." He gave her another quick, reflective look. "Chantal won't even travel in the same car as me," he went on, his voice rough with amusement. "She wouldn't even in Tunis, if you remember?"

Katherine did.

"It isn't the speed exactly," she explained. "It's the lack of protection."

He appeared to find this reasonable, for he nodded and said briefly,

"It's quite safe really. Relax a bit and you'll find you quite enjoy it."

She tried it and found that he was quite right. Besides, at rock bottom she was pretty sure that she could rely on him not to do anything that would endanger anyone else's life. He had the right hands, she thought. Strong, gentle hands that she had liked the feel of against her face. She looked down at her own hands and blushed. *No,* she told herself firmly, he would *not* think the same about hers.

She had thought the steppe lands were poor, but she was soon to realise that they were comparatively rich. They were being reclaimed and planted with eucalyptus trees first, because they didn't object so strongly to the salt, and then with olive trees and other crops. It was planned too to shade the long miles of the roads with handsome trees to make driving more pleasant for the tourists and other travellers. Sometimes they would pass a water barrel being hauled along by a mule with a man sitting on the top, going on his rounds to give the trees their weekly watering.

But soon the land was to deteriorate still further until the soil was little more than sand and the olive and eucalyptus trees gave way to the wild esparto grass that was casually picked by the passing Bedouin and sent to the paper mills all over the world.

They passed in turn an agricultural school, a flock of wild pigeons, and yet more saplings, protected from the sun by little shelters of palm-leaves. They crossed some of the dry river beds too, the rains of a few weeks earlier now no more than a memory and a few damp places in the sand below them. It was hard to believe that these same beds had been swirling torrents of water such a short time before, but the occasional washed away bridge bore silent witness to the force of these short, violent storms that occasionally swirled through this near-desert.

Dr. Kreistler would drive the Land Rover straight into the *wadi* and out the other side with the same fierce concentration he brought to everything else. It was left to Katherine to close her eyes to shut out the terrifying drifts of sand that lay to either side of the temporary pass, a pass so narrow that it didn't seem possible that anything as wide as the Land Rover could possibly cross over it.

But she became accustomed to the ordeal in time and even began to enjoy it. There was something satisfying about the miles of yellow sand and the terra-cotta mountains slashed by vivid purple shadows, or the wide, flat and completely white salt lakes that would fill with water every winter and dry out every summer, useless, as even the salt was not gathered for export.

They drove straight through Sbeitla, leaving the ruined Roman city to one side and dodging the multitude of little boys who tried to sell them Roman coins for whatever they could get.

"Can you wait until we reach Gafsa before we stop for some coffee?" Dr. Kreistler asked her.

She stirred herself out of the silent reverie she had fallen into.

"Yes, of course," she said.

He gave her a quick smile of encouragement and she smiled back. She could feel the hot sun on her flesh and she dreaded to think of how burnt she would be when the sun went down and she would feel the full effect of its heat against her tender skin.

More alarming still was the sudden change in the weather. The sky was still the same steely blue above them, but all round the horizon it looked a dirty yellow and thick with dust.

"Are we going to have a storm?" she asked fearfully.

He laughed.

"A very little one! More dust, I'm afraid. It's just the wind playing with the loose sand."

It made for a grim few miles of driving, though. There was sand everywhere, blowing across the road, in their hair, in their eyes and, worst of all, in their mouths, gritty and particularly nasty between their teeth.

Dr. Kreistler threw her an anxious glance every now and again, but Katherine was accustomed to being uncomfortable and she knew how to ride out such a situation, letting the worst of it blow over her head, and not making a fuss about the inevitable.

"I have some chocolate," he said at last. "If you would care to look for it in my pocket."

She felt shy and rather ridiculous going through his pockets. He seemed to keep the oddest things in them — anything from a piece of string and a safety pin to a single, rather elderly potato that was showing every sign of sprouting in the near future.

"It must be on the other side," she told him.

He slowed down, put a hand in his pocket and tossed it over to her. She ripped open the paper and returned half of it to him.

"Good?" he asked her.

She laughed.

"The sand makes a novel filling," she said.

It seemed no time after that that they came into the outskirts of Gafsa, an ugly little town in the centre of the phosphate belt. All the streets were garlanded with flags in readiness for Independence Day and the people had come out in a body and stood in clusters on the edge of the road, their excitement so great that it was almost tangible in the sand-filled atmosphere.

"Do you want to stop?" the doctor asked her.

"What's happening?" she countered. But there was no doubt that she wanted to stop. She was half out of the car before he had even parked it off the road, and had joined the crowd, her eyes alight with eager anticipation.

"What is it?" she asked a man she found beside her.

He stood back to allow her to pass to the front so that she would have a better view.

"It's a *fantasia, madame,*" he replied. He pointed out across the sand into the grey-yellow dust. "Look over there!"

The Bedouin horsemen came pounding down towards them, their rifles blazing and their horses responding to their lightest touch. They looked magnificent in their long white burnouses, their extravagantly embroidered belts and shoulder straps, and the long drapes of green and scarlet that flew out behind them from the back of their saddles.

They came to a resounding halt within a few feet of the crowd and steadied into a sober walk as the band started up with pounding beat and ear-splitting trumpets and bagpipes.

Katherine looked round for the doctor and found him close behind her.

"So you like this sort of thing?" he asked her.

She nodded her head, suddenly shy.

"Don't you?"

But there was no need to wait for his answer. He obviously did. He stood on a hillock of sand, his hands negligently thrust into his pockets, and he looked relaxed. Even when the guns exploded over his head he remained quite calm, exchanging a word of laughter with the leader of the horsemen.

The horses retreated again into the distance and the crowds pressed forward, the children thrusting their way through their elders' legs into the front where they could see. Katherine held her breath, waiting for them to come again in another wave of colour and audacity, but this time they came singly, one standing in his saddle, another swivelled right down behind his horse, and yet another using his galloping mount to leapfrog over, from one side to the other.

The accident seemed to happen in a matter of seconds. One moment the small boy was standing in front of her and in another he had rushed forward towards the horses and was flat on his back with the huge Arab stallion pawing madly at the air over his head.

Katherine ran towards him as fast as she could, pulling him away from those wicked hooves. There was a splash of blood on his head and he was crying. For an instant she was as frightened as he was, and then she pulled herself together and tried to see how extensively he was hurt. He had a nasty cut on the back of his head, but she could find nothing else to worry about. He was more scared than hurt, she decided, and she comforted him in the easy, laughing way that she had comforted a hundred other frightened children.

He didn't know what she was saying, but he recognised the tone and smiled back at her.

"Pardon, madame," he muttered.

Katherine felt strong hands push her to one side and recognised them immediately as Dr. Kreistler's.

"He's not badly hurt," she told him in her most professional tones. "Just a scratch on the back of his head."

The doctor examined the boy for himself and then stood up, looking down at her from a great height. Then without a word he turned on his heel and walked back to the Land Rover. A second later when she looked over to him, she saw him impatiently looking at his watch again.

"Oh, bother everything!" she said crossly. Couldn't she do anything right as far as he was concerned?

The mother of the child was dressed all in black

and couldn't speak a single word of French. She managed to make her gratitude clear with a flood of Arabic and tears that Katherine couldn't stem at all until she brought her own handkerchief to wipe the woman's eyes. She knew just how the woman felt, but there was nothing more that she could do. They looked deep into each other's eyes and smiled in sudden, mute understanding.

"Besslama," the woman murmured at last.

That at least was one word Katherine had heard before.

"Besslama," she replied gently, and lost herself in the crowd, fighting her way back to the Land Rover and Dr. Kreistler.

If she had thought that he had driven fast before, it was nothing to the pace that he set now. He stopped on the top of a bridge and checked all the tyres in readiness for the sharp deterioration of the road ahead.

"Hold on!" he told her briefly.

She did, as though her life depended on it. It seemed to her that there were some parts of the road that they never touched at all — this was not driving at all, it was low flying! And all the time the doctor drove he was silent, angrily silent in a way that intimidated her. What could she possibly have done to annoy him so much?

She could see the green of the date palms of Tozeur long before she realised that this was the oasis where they would be stopping to eat. When they got nearer she could see the narrow streets of the small town and the allotments that were spread out in the cool of the trees. After the unbroken, sand-coloured landscape they had passed through, it seemed a miracle to see fruit trees in blossom, and even a very English standard rose.

Dr. Kreistler was obviously well known at the

hotel. Even the boys selling dates and Arab sandals in the entrance ran forward to greet him and to lead him into the hotel. Katherine followed on behind him. She was stiff and shaken after those last punishing miles and she was hungry too, but when she found herself in the dining-room, sitting opposite the doctor, she didn't want to eat anything.

"You'd better eat something," he told her dryly. "We still have the Chott Djerid to cross — a dried-out salt lake," he added when he saw that it meant nothing to her. "Sidi Behn Ahmed is just on the other side."

She picked up her knife and fork and tried the dish they had set in front of her. She might have been in Paris and not on the edge of the Sahara at all, for the food was truly excellent but definitely French!

Dr. Kreistler waited for her to finish, and then, with that suddenness that he appeared to be the master of, he smiled at her.

"And now, Miss Katherine Lane," he said, quite quietly but without the slightest doubt that he was going to be answered, "tell me all about it."

She tell him! It was he who had been so angry! He whose moods changed so rapidly that they frightened her! He —

"I'm a nurse," she said bleakly. "I nursed Monsieur de Hallet just before he died."

She couldn't see what he was thinking. When he looked down his eyebrows completely hid his eyes and she could only see them and the firm line of his chin.

"I'm a nurse," she said again, and her voice trembled slightly.

"Qualifications?" he snapped out.

She told him, her confidence growing as she did so. She was a good nurse and she knew it.

There was a silence after she had finished, and

then he looked up, his eyes bright and challenging.

"Why wasn't I told?" he demanded.

Uncomfortably she sipped at her drink.

"I thought you knew at first," she said. "It wasn't any secret. Then afterwards it seemed too late to tell you. I mean —"

"You mean that you enjoyed seeing me making a fool of myself telling you that a little work was what you needed?"

She was horrified. Was that how it had seemed to him?

"Oh, no, it wasn't that!" she exclaimed. "Work *was* what I needed. I've never had nothing to do before. And anyway, I have to work. I can't afford not to."

He laughed with frank disbelief.

"How extravagant have you decided to be?" he asked her.

She began to tell him about the canning plant, her enthusiasm for the idea spilling over into her words.

"And so you won't be drawing from the estate yourself?"

She shook her head.

"Not a penny if I can help it! Monsieur de Hallet left it to me as a kind of trust, if you see what I mean."

"Is that so?" he drawled, but his smile was kindly. "I think you should know that Edouard didn't like his young relatives particularly. I hardly think he would want you to manage the properties for their exclusive benefit."

"No," she agreed solemnly. She had not forgotten that they hadn't even bothered to write to the old man. "No, not for them. For the country as a whole. It's silly that whenever there's a glut the oranges have to be left to rot." She chuckled suddenly. "Why, it might be the beginning of a whole new industry!" she said.

He smiled with her and, for the moment, she was completely happy.

"It might indeed!" he laughed.

The narrow trail across the Chott Djerid had only recently dried out and the salt lay deep in patches, completely white, waiting for the unwary to drive into it and sink through the brittle crust until the wheels spun helplessly and it was a major operation to get the car moving again. The doctor had driven across it so often that the hazards no longer seemed to affect him. Every now and again he would stop the Land Rover, climb out and spread two long strips of canvas in front of the wheels, drive over them and quietly pick them up again. Sometimes Katherine would help him, but more often than not he would wave her back to her seat, and, truth to tell, she wasn't at all sorry, for she was tired right through to the very marrow of her bones.

The first glimpse of Sidi Behn Ahmed showed green in the distance beyond the white of the salt. The sun was sinking rapidly in a blaze of red and orange and a lonely *marabout,* the tomb of some holy man, stood high above the village, quite pink in the evening light. This, Katherine supposed, was the *marabout* the oasis had been called after. They left it behind on their left and started down the long straight street of Berber houses, the geometrical patterns of the bricks almost hurting the eyes, so clear was the atmosphere.

"The hospital is over there," Dr. Kreistler told her, pointing out a large Western-style building that flew the red crescent over it for all to see. "Your house is just round the corner from it."

The date palms clustered thickly on either side of the road, obscuring her view of the houses, and then they came out into the sandy clearing in front of the hospital and she could see her own house for the first time.

It was as yellow as the sand that surrounded it and built on the Arab principle of the central square with all the rooms built round it. From the outside all that could be seen were the tall flat walls and one or two windows, too high for the stranger to peer into. Katherine looked at it for a long moment and thought how very different it was from the luxury of the house at Hammamet.

The doctor seemed to be thinking very much the same thing.

"Will you be content here, by yourself?" he asked as he stopped the car outside her door and applied the brake.

She looked about her, delighted by everything she saw.

"I think so," she said.

She stepped down from the Land Rover and almost stumbled. In a second he had taken her arm.

"I should be happier if you had the de Hallets with you," he muttered. "Go inside and have a hot bath."

She smiled a little uncertainly.

"I'll do that." She turned to him abruptly. "I haven't thanked you for coming to Kairouan, but I am grateful, Dr. Kreistler."

"You won't be when I have you working sixteen hours a day and then call you out at night! You won't be able to bear the sight of me!"

"I'm accustomed to hard work," she replied simply.

He put her suitcases in her doorway and jumped back into the Land Rover.

"I could still wish that you had brought Chantal with you," he said.

And not entirely for her sake, she thought wryly.

If he could only know how very glad she was to be away from the other girl! She wasn't good enough for him, of that she was quite certain. But then perhaps he didn't mind if *she* did nothing all day. Perhaps he even liked it. She watched him drive away, across to the hospital, and sighed. Then she turned her back on him, picked up her suitcases and walked into the house.

It was cool inside and the darkness was a joy after the endless glare of the salt and the sand. Katherine put her cases down in the small hall and went out into the courtyard beyond. A few flowering creepers clung to the pillars and a fountain played in the centre, making the whole place cool and pleasant. There were little singing birds too in all the corners, twittering excitedly in competition with the water. It was cool and calm and very lovely.

She was still standing by the fountain when the houseboy came out to flit the rooms for the night and to close the netting windows to keep the insects and the flies outside.

"Madame!" he exclaimed nervously.

She smiled at him.

"I arrived with the doctor, as you see," she told him. "Will you take my bags to my room?"

He glanced at her, looking quickly away again, standing there in a mute, embarrassed silence.

"Didn't you get my message?" Katherine asked.

He nodded his head violently.

"But there is nothing ready, *madame,*" he burst out. "The other *madame* will never allow me to prepare any of the rooms unless she tells me to personally. I am very sorry, *madame.*"

Katherine was so angry she could hardly speak. She might have left Chantal at Hammamet, but it seemed that her tentacles reached right down here to Sidi Behn Ahmed. Why? Why should she make such a stupid rule?

"I am sorry, *madame*," the houseboy repeated hopefully.

"It's not your fault," Katherine said evenly. "Please make up a bed for me now, though — in the *best* room!" she added thoughtfully.

The shocked look he gave her made her want to laugh. It was silly to have been so annoyed, even for a moment. There was probably some very good reason for Chantal making such a rule. She would probably quite soon find out exactly what it was.

She was just going to bed when the doctor called in to see if she had everything she wanted. He glanced about him with an appreciative eye and accepted the drink she gave him.

"I am sorry to come still so dusty and dirty," he said, "but I wanted to make sure that you locked all the doors and that you are comfortable." He tossed the drink down his throat as though he had been drinking vodka and not good Scotch whisky. "I must go," he said immediately, and walked rapidly to the front door. Katherine went with him, wondering if he ever paused in his work to look after himself for a while.

"Goodnight, Doctor," she said.

He walked through the open door, looking suddenly tired and dispirited.

"It doesn't seem right to have this house open without Chantal here," he sighed. "I'll see you in the morning."

Katherine shut the door after him and rammed the heavy locks home. Botheration take Chantal, she thought. It's Chantal this and Chantal that, and I don't even *like* Chantal! But she too felt that she was trespassing as she went to her room. She even imagined for a moment that she could smell the other girl's distinctive perfume left behind from when *she* had inhabited the best bedroom. But that, at least, was easily remedied. She flung open both the windows, pressing the shutters right back against the wall and the scent of the creepers in the courtyard down below came rushing in to meet her. It might have been Chantal's room in the past, but now it was hers!

CHAPTER SIX

IT HAD been cold in the night, but as soon as the sun got up humans and animals alike crept from one patch of shade to another in an effort to keep cool. It was the favourite occupation of the men to throw a couple of highly-coloured camel blankets down on to the street and brew tea on a tiny charcoal fire so that they could sit and gossip the hours away in comparative comfort.

Katherine had been awakened by the noise at a very early hour. At first she couldn't think what on earth was happening, and hurried into her clothes at break-neck speed so as not to miss anything. But when she went out she discovered that it was no more than the weekly market. A whole caravan of camels had come into the village during the night and the tall, extra-ordinary beasts had been seated in a long line by their owners and were now being fed by hand on a mixture of leaves and prickly pear.

There were flocks of sheep too, fat with brown patches across their shoulders and buttocks and the occasional flash of black. Some of the flocks were mixed with goats, giving the scene a Biblical quality that was borne out by the dress of the people. In complete contrast was the backdrop of the hospital, a completely modern building, with an even more modern signpost outside it, giving its name in Arabic and French and with a large scarlet crescent at each end.

"Hullo, you're up early!" a voice called out to her across the square, and she saw the doctor leaning against one of the camels with his medicine bag in his hand.

"Are you starting your rounds?" she asked him,

laughing. She was thinking of the soberly clad doctors she had known at home, quite different from this man whose khaki trousers were stained with engine grease and who wore his shirt outside his pants for the added coolness it gave him.

"I'm off to visit one of the clinics," he agreed. "I'll see you when I get back."

Katherine remembered the notices she had seen on the hospital door, forbidding any unauthorised person to enter.

"May I take a look round?" she asked him.

He grinned at her.

"Can't you wait to get into harness, Nurse?" he teased her.

She found that she didn't like him calling her Nurse any more than she had liked him calling her Miss Lane, and thought that she must be getting very hard to please.

"I shall be glad to have something to do," she said primly.

His eyes mocked her.

"I can't think now why I didn't recognise you immediately for what you are," he told her. "I should have known the instant I saw you running off with my medicines!"

She held out her hands to him.

"I think it was these that bluffed you," she reminded him dryly. "I seem to remember you thought they had never seen a day's work!"

He didn't look in the least repentant.

"I can see they are your biggest vanity," he agreed smoothly. "So soft and smooth and pretty, yes?"

She flushed angrily.

"I hardly ever do anything to them at all!" she denied indignantly. "An occasional hand-cream, that's all."

His eyes laughed at her.

"It is not a crime to look after one's hands, Nurse,"

he retorted, and his lopsided smile was more mocking than ever. "And yes, you may have a look over the hospital. Tell the head nurse I sent you." He glanced quickly at his watch. "I must be off," he said abruptly, and vanished down the street, his long legs covering the ground at a pace that Katherine could only envy.

She was smiling as she turned to go towards the hospital. Dear God, she wondered, how did he ever keep it up?

The familiar smell of disinfectant greeted her nostrils as she pushed open the doors of the hospital. For her it was a comfortable smell, reminding her of London and the world there that she had known so well. In comparison this hospital was very small and compact, but it was none the less scrupulously clean with the same wide corridors and the same underlying hum of activity.

The head nurse was a man. He came towards her down the long, green-walled corridor, looking tall and rather remote in his white uniform. He greeted her solemnly.

"The doctor told me you would be coming," he said with a smile, "but I did not think today. You drove a long way yesterday, I thought you would be still asleep!"

She laughed with him.

"I couldn't wait," she admitted. "You have a very fine hospital here."

"We are fortunate." He sighed. "But we still have many things that we need. It is difficult to build hospitals everywhere at once, and we are a long way from Tunis."

He led the way, as he was speaking, towards the first room and started on the tour of his domain. Katherine was impressed by the way they had made use of everything that had been given to them. The radiography equipment was modern and extensive.

"There is much tuberculosis down here in the south," the nurse explained simply. "You will see that it is in the theatre that we need more modern equipment so badly. Fortunately we don't often have to operate down here. We can fly our patients out to one of the big hospitals."

But it was the wards that appealed to Katherine most. She cast a professional eye over the beds and saw immediately that they were properly made and that the patients had been made as comfortable as possible. And what patients! The men had clung to their headdresses and sat on their beds looking like so many camel-drivers in the gloomy light, and the women wound their veils tightly about them, or, if they were Bedouin, stared suspiciously out at her over their dresses of brightly coloured silk and tattooed cheeks. The silence was only broken when they tried to leave one of the wards, and then a chorus of cries would call them back again so that the patients could have another long look at this strange woman who had come amongst them.

Altogether she spent a very pleasant morning there. It was easy to follow the treatments that were being given, for they were all written up in French, and the brand names of the French drugs were mostly ones that were familiar to her. She could see how important the clinics were, for in a district such as this, prevention was much better than cure. Simple hygiene and antenatal clinics would have to come first, slowly educating the people away from their own customs which were a mixture of indifference and ceremonial to ward off the evil eye.

The sun was high in the sky when she went back to her own house and it was unbearably hot. She found the houseboy lying full-length under the palm-tree in the courtyard and hadn't the heart to disturb him. Instead she went to the kitchen and made herself a long, very cold fruit drink and drank it very slowly, willing herself to feel cooler. Perhaps Dr. Kreistler would take her to one of his clinics tomorrow.

After lunch she found a light breeze had got up, and, determined to make the most of it, she took a book and ventured into the depths of the oasis. The date palms clustered round the hundred and one little springs, sometimes separated by cliffs of sandstone from the top of which one could see the splashes of blue and white houses and the endless miles of rolling sand beyond. She chose her place carefully and settled down to read. Below her she could see the chains of allotments and the blossoms of an apricot tree. She lay back and smiled at the little puffs of white cloud that hurried across the sky, and within a few seconds she was fast asleep.

She was awakened by a hand gently shaking her shoulder. She sat up with a start and found the doctor sitting on the ground beside her.

"Aren't you afraid of snakes and scorpions, Nurse?" he asked her.

She gave him a rueful look.

"Terrified," she admitted. "But I'm afraid I forgot that there were such things."

He lay flat on his back beside her, completely relaxed in a way that she had never previously seen him.

"This is good," he said. "I hadn't realised how tired I was."

She was silent, not liking to intrude on his few moments of peace. Moreover she was a little embarrassed that he should have caught her sleeping and aware that the uneven ground had left a pattern on her cheek and that a few twigs had somehow got caught up in her plaits. She thought of Chantal, immaculate and chic, and sighed. She would never, *never* be able to emulate her, even if she wanted to. A little black beetle ran across the sand beside her and she hurried it on its way by blowing on it. When she turned round again, she was aware that the doctor was watching her.

"Are there many scorpions — and *things* around here?" she asked him.

He laughed. It was amazing how good he was to look at, she thought. She liked his smooth brown throat and the way his hair grew away from his temples.

"Oh, lots! Especially *things!*" He reached out a hand and pulled a burr off the edge of her skirt. "Don't you wish those dates were ripe now?" he asked her. "So that we could reach up and take a few instead of having to go all the way home for some?"

She shook her head.

"I like to see the flower. It looks so unlikely."

She looked down at him, leaning up on one elbow so that she could see him better. His eyes met hers, and she could feel herself blushing scarlet. Oh dear, this would never do! What on earth was she doing dallying with Dr. Peter Kreistler on the edge of Paradise? She turned away from him quickly and buried her face in her arms. She could feel the hot sun against her back and she knew the instant that his shadow came between her and it — long before she felt his breath on the back of her neck.

Then the silence was shattered by the thud of feet running towards them and a group of children came over the top of the hill, yelling for all they were worth.

"Doctori! Doctori! Doctori!"

The moment before might never have been. Dr. Kreistler was on his feet in an instant, his whole attention given to the children. Their eyes dark and tragic, they poured out their story to him.

"I'll need you, Katherine," he called out, and he

strode off down the hill without a single backward glance.

Katherine ran after him, her book forgotten, doing her best to restore some order to her appearance as she went. Her hair was in acute danger of coming down and the pins refused to hold it properly, so that she was obliged to stop and anchor it more firmly. When she had done, the doctor was almost out of sight and she had to make a dash to catch up with him.

He came to a stop outside the door of a single house, set a little apart from any of the others, and rapped on the door, pushing it open without bothering to wait for an answer.

Katherine arrived hot and breathless behind him, wondering what on earth her ex-Ward Sister would have said if she could have seen her now. The doctor took a long, critical look at her and started into the house.

"Wait here until I send for you," he commanded her. "And this time *do as you're told!*" he added over his shoulder.

She stood on the doorstep, rigid with indignation, and waited for him. It was so unfair! When had she ever not carried out the orders of a doctor well and efficiently? Just because she hadn't obeyed his telegram and stayed in Hammamet but had decided to travel alone!

The doctor came out again with the owner of the house, a scowling Berber, with tight lips and a fanatical look in his eyes.

"If you don't your wife will surely die!" Dr. Kreistler shouted at him. He was brusque, almost rude, in his impatience. Katherine couldn't ever imagine him suffering fools gladly, but she couldn't help feeling that this was not the way to get the man to change his mind.

"Then die she must!" the man retorted. But there

89

were tears in his eyes even as he said it. It was a bitter moment for him.

"And you will have killed her!" the doctor pursued him relentlessly.

Katherine took a step forward, her eyes soft with pity.

"May I see your wife?" she asked the man in French.

He saw that she was a woman and therefore harmless, and nodded.

"See her if you will, but she is already dead to me."

Katherine didn't dare look in the doctor's direction as she stepped into the house. He made a movement as if to stop her and then stood back a trifle uncertainly.

"It might not be very pleasant," he warned her.

She looked at him then, directly in the eyes.

"I've seen unpleasant things before," she told him quietly.

But she had never seen anything like the scene that met her eyes in the courtyard of the house. Keening women stood in groups, weeping and wailing and generally making so much noise that Katherine could feel it like a solid wall in front of her. Which one was the patient she had no means of knowing.

The house itself was very much like her own, if a little smaller, and instead of a date-palm in the courtyard, there was a well with high walls all round it to prevent the children from falling in. Katherine went over to it and stood there, surveying the scene until someone should notice her.

In the end it was a young, very obviously pregnant, girl who came towards her, her eyes bright with curiosity. She said something in Arabic and put out a hand to finger Katherine's dress. It was clear that she liked it, for she smiled and touched it again.

"Whose house is this?" Katherine asked her.

But she only giggled, not understanding a word. It was only the men who could speak French. The women spoke Arabic or Berber or a mixture of both and still found Europeans an exciting novelty.

Katherine pointed to the well and pretended she wanted a drink. Perhaps that, she thought, would make the girl find her hostess. At first she only laughed, but she nodded her head with comprehension and disappeared into one of the darkened rooms that led off the courtyard. Katherine followed her quickly, for she was afraid that once she let her out of her sight she wouldn't recognise her again.

But she had only gone to get a glass from a tall dresser that stood against one of the whitewashed walls. Katherine went over to the bed that stood in the corner only to find it empty. Bewildered, the girl followed her, watching her closely and obviously wondering what she was going to do next.

"Lala," she said, pointing to herself.

"Katherine," Katherine responded.

"Ah!" The girl giggled and shifted her veil to show a cloud of hennaed hair beneath, her dark eyes never leaving Katherine's face for an instant. Then suddenly she seemed to make up her mind, and, grabbing Katherine's hand, she led her into the next-door bedroom and stood waiting in the entrance, her face a mask of fear.

Katherine approached the bed with the confidence her training had given her. An old crone stood over it, murmuring incantations and waving a piece of paper over the girl who lay, writhing in agony, beside her.

There was a hushed silence as Katherine drew back the bedclothes and smiled reassuringly at the young mother-to-be. A hundred black eyes tried to see what she was doing from the doorway, pushing and shoving each other to get to the front, but at least no longer keening as they had been before.

It was a breech baby. She was as sure of that as she could be without any proper equipment. Silently she replaced the bedclothes and turned to face the wall of women in the doorway. They stood back to allow her to pass, padding after her as she made her way through the courtyard and out into the sunshine in the street.

"Well?" the doctor demanded.

"It's a breech," she said briefly, "and the mother is very tired. She'll have to be taken to the hospital. We couldn't possibly cope here."

"*We?*" he repeated briefly. "I'm not even allowed to see her!"

She knew a moment's panic.

"But I couldn't do it," she said helplessly.

"You'll have to!" he retorted grimly.

"Then you'll have to explain to Lala how to help me," she told him. "I will *not* have that old woman breathing down the back of my neck!"

He smiled, and the look she had first noticed at the airport was back in his eyes.

"I'll tell her," he agreed. "Bring her out here to me."

Lala came willingly enough. She enveloped herself in her white woollen veil until only one eye was showing and followed Katherine out into the street. Her air of importance vanished, however, when she saw the doctor. She listened to all that he had to say, her one visible eye growing as round as a saucer. Dr. Kreistler pointed to the husband and she followed his finger with a look of outraged contempt.

In silence the doctor handed Katherine his medical bag.

"I'll be here," he called after her. "I'll be here all the time."

It seemed to her that the suffocating atmosphere had grown worse in the last few moments. Little prickles of heat all down her back made her uncomfortable and irritable, but it fell from her as she saw her patient. She made a signal to Lala and the girl pushed the old woman out with a flood of words that cowed most of the rest of the audience as well.

And then they set to work.

Lala was delighted with the baby. She wrapped it up and placed it in the waiting wedding basket beside the bed, laughing and cooing at it all the while. The husband should be pleased as well, Katherine thought grimly. It was a boy.

She herself was tired out. It was the heat, she thought, the suffocating heat, and the endless chatter from the women outside. For one horrible moment she thought she was going to faint. She watched Lala tuck the infant in and laughed as she patted herself and pointed to the child. It was so very obvious that Lala was pregnant that she certainly didn't need telling! She hoped that her husband was more modern in his views, for she liked the girl, with her gentle hands and curious eyes.

Dr. Kreistler's bag shut easily, and it was pleasant to feel its solid weight in her hand as she went out into the courtyard. It was almost as though she had a part of him with her. She was surprised to discover that she had been conscious of his presence all through the difficult birth. He had said that he would wait, and in some ridiculous way it had given her confidence to know that he would be there when she came out.

But it was a long time before she was allowed to escape. The women crowded round her, offering her sweetmeats and mint tea and trying desperately to make her feel at home. They got out the very best perfume they had and poured it over her hands, laughing out loud when she put some behind her ears instead of pouring it down the front of her dress as they would have done.

93

They were amazed too by her long fair hair. The bolder among them would put out a hand and touch it, giggling and discussing it amongst themselves. Lala tried to persuade her to take it down, and it was Katherine's turn to be shy as she shook her head. But the Berber girl considered herself a friend and wouldn't take no for an answer. With eager fingers she pulled out the pins that held it and shook it free so that it fell in corn-coloured profusion around Katherine's shoulders.

There was a gasp of pure admiration from the women. They led her to the one chair in the house, and, a little reluctantly, she sat in it. She wanted to go home, to change her dress and to somehow get cool. And she wanted to see Dr. Kreistler. She wanted that more than anything. But she knew it would be the worst thing she could do to offend these women. If she could once win their confidence they would insist upon attending the clinic no matter what their husbands said, if it was only out of curiosity.

Lala sat on the floor beside her and basked in her reflected glory. She showed Katherine how to eat the honey-sweet doughnuts without getting them all over her dress and she guarded her from the others with her quick tongue and lightning laughter.

At last Katherine felt that she could make her escape. She retreated backwards to the doorway, shaking hands with a dozen that were eagerly extended to her.

She was terribly conscious of her loosened hair and her distinctly dishevelled appearance. She stood in the entrance to the house, blinking in the sunlight and taking deep breaths of the unbelievably fresh air, trying to restore some order before the doctor saw her.

She was unlucky, however, for he stepped forward immediately and grasped both her hands in his, swinging her round to face him.

"How did it go?" he asked her.

She couldn't bring herself to meet his eyes, but her lips twitched with amusement.

"Mother and child are both doing nicely," she said. "As well as can be expected, anyway," she added on a more doubtful note.

His eyes swept up her, fastening on her hair.

"And the nurse?" he laughed.

She bit her lip and tried to free her hands so that she could plait it up again into her usual staid style, but he wouldn't allow her.

"I like it," he told her. "I like the way it ripples." He smiled at her outraged face. "You're tired, Nurse," he said more formally. "It's time I took you home to rest."

But she found that her temper was still very much alive under her fatigue.

"It's nothing more than *ignorance!*" she said stormily. "These women need to be taught some simple hygiene more than anything else —"

He took her by the arm and started to lead her away.

"We are doing our best. We show them films and instruct them in every way we can. A lot of them do come to the clinics now. Especially the Berber women, they have a little more freedom than their Arab sisters."

"And I suppose that girl is an Arab!" Katherine exclaimed angrily.

"Her husband is," he replied quietly.

She tossed her hair back behind her shoulders and peered up at him, a little nonplussed.

"I don't know how you can stay so calm about it," she said at last.

He laughed.

"My dear Katherine, I am not calm! I burn with the same indignation that you do. Only I know also the value of a little patience. All these things are so new to these people. It is only six years since they had to take responsibility for their own lives. They cannot do everything at once."

"But something *is* being done?" she insisted.

He nodded gravely.

"But this is no time to talk about it," he said. "Go home and get a bath. That scent they have smothered you in is a trifle overpowering!"

She smiled up at him.

"I rather like it!" she said provocatively.

But he only took his bag from her and gave her a little shake.

"Go home, Katherine," he repeated.

The camel market was almost over when she strolled back through the open square. Only a trickle of people and animals were left, sitting quietly in the evening sun, their baracans wrapped tightly round them. The old men were playing dominoes or draughts and indulging in the soothing ritual of making tea on their little charcoal stoves. They glanced up as she passed and nodded a greeting, their eyes following her every step of the way. So they had already been told about the birth, she reflected, and wondered what they thought of it all. A small boy offered to sell her some outrageously coloured imitation Iceland poppies, and his face fell when she said no.

"Perhaps some dates, then?" he pleaded. *"Deglats Nour!"* he coaxed her. "Fingers of Light. You can't buy any better. They will only grow in the oasis here, where they can have their roots in water and their leaves in the burning sun!"

She bought a box, knowing that she didn't like dates very much. She could offer a few to the doctor, she thought, and knew that was really why she had bought them. She gave the boy a note from her purse and waved away the change. She must be mad! She carried the box into the house and took it straight into the kitchen, hiding it at the very back of the store cupboard, hoping that she would never have to see it ever again. She was not, repeat *not,* going to fall in love with the doctor!

It was inevitable that the box of dates should have been brought out to decorate the dinner table that night. Her houseboy enjoyed the full ritual of European dining and would lay the table with infinite care, even placing a finger bowl beside her place when he brought the fruit. Katherine sat and hated it all through the first course so that she didn't even notice the letter that had been put beside her plate until the Tunisian stamp caught her eye, twice as large as any English stamp and with a jaunty-looking female riding a dolphin on it.

She didn't know the handwriting. It was large and feminine and surprisingly difficult to read. Katherine opened it slowly and turned immediately to the signature. It was from Chantal.

She read through the truculent demand for more money with dogged care and penned her answer before she had time to weaken and change her mind. There was no more money, and the de Hallets would simply have to manage like everyone else. She was glad though when the houseboy picked up the addressed envelope with the rest of the dishes and offered to post it for her. She felt mean and prissy, and the canning plant seemed very, very far away.

CHAPTER SEVEN

KATHERINE began to fall into a routine at the hospital. There were six nurses there besides herself, and all of them had trained in Tunis and were proud of the fact that they no longer had to go to France to learn their profession. Four of them were men and two were women, and they were the most enthusiastic and dedicated people Katherine had ever met. They made her very welcome, finding a multitude of tasks for her to do that didn't involve too many language difficulties.

"You should learn Arabic," they told her. "Dr. Kreistler learned it in less than a year. He would help you, I'm sure."

But she didn't like to ask him. Instead she asked Lala. The Berber girl had found her book, where she had left it on top of the hill, and brought it to the house in person in the middle of one particularly hot afternoon.

Katherine found her sitting in a little huddle in the middle of the courtyard, listening to the transistor set she had hidden under her veil. The houseboy had shouted at her and had finally tried to push her bodily outside, but Lala had continued to sit there, calmly swaying in time to the music and waiting for Katherine to notice her.

"Bring tea," Katherine told the houseboy sternly. "And cakes," she added a shade more doubtfully. She wasn't sure if Lala would try any strange foods and she regretted that she hadn't any Arabic sweetmeats to offer her.

The houseboy lingered, plainly reluctant to serve a woman of his own kind. In his eyes she should have been serving him.

"Go quickly, Ali," Katherine said. "Lala is my guest."

Lala giggled, allowing her veil to fall back as Ali departed. With great care she placed the radio on the ground beside her and turned it off, eagerly looking about her. Katherine offered her one of the light wicker chairs that stood under the palm-tree, but she shook her head, preferring to sit on the ground.

The cakes were a great success. Lala ate them all with a fierce concentration that alternated with the inevitable giggles that broke from her at the slightest provocation. She tried drinking lemon tea as Katherine was doing, but hated the faintly bitter taste and hastily ladled spoonfuls of sugar into her cup and drank the resulting syrup, her dark eyes full of laughter as they peered over the edge of the cup.

When she had done, Katherine showed her over the house, and then her first Arabic lesson began. By the time Lala left they both knew that this was going to be a regular feature of their days, and Katherine was already wondering if she could remember how to make such things as coconut-ice and fudge, or anything else that would be sweet enough to appeal to the other girl.

It was only just as she was leaving that Lala produced the book and gave it to her, with a pretended indifference that dismayed Katherine. It was the first time that she had realised that Lala, like most of the other women of Tunisia, couldn't read or write, and that she envied anyone who could. A hundred other women wouldn't have cared at all, but Lala had an intense curiosity about anything that came her way. Lala, in fact, was a darling.

"Salaam 'aleikum!"
"Wa 'aleikum es salaam!" Katherine responded automatically.

"So it's true what they say in the market place, you are learning Arabic!"

Katherine looked up and smiled at the doctor. He was leaning negligently against her front door, his eyes faintly amused, and she was quite terribly glad to see him.

"I've learned a few words," she admitted. *"Not* enough to become the *on dit* of the oasis, I should have said," she added ruefully. "I find it terribly difficult."

He came right inside, scooped up a chair with one foot, and sat down in it, facing her. His eyes wandered round the courtyard and she was glad she had taken the trouble to make Ali clean the whole place that morning. The smell of polish mixed pleasantly with the heavy scent of the creepers and there wasn't a grain of sand anywhere. Tomorrow it would all be back, creeping in through every door, on the soles of one's shoes and in the creases of one's clothes, but it was nice to be without it, even for a few minutes.

"It seems different in here," he said at last. "It's more peaceful than I remembered it."

Was it? Katherine wondered. It probably was so, for she couldn't imagine that there would ever be much peace around Chantal.

"I make you free of it," she said. "You're always welcome here."

He looked surprised and then a little anxious.

"How long have you been here?" he asked. "A fortnight? I suppose I have been neglecting you?"

Katherine shook her head.

"I didn't come here to be entertained," she reminded him. "I came to work. It's pleasant, though, to see you doing nothing for a few minutes!"

He leaned back in his chair and smiled.

"I could do with a drink," he told her. "A very long, very cold drink."

She got him it herself, squashing the cold citrus fruit straight out of the refrigerator and fishing out the few pips that had fallen into the glass. She added a teaspoonful of water and filled up the glass with bottled soda water. When she took it to him her hand was trembling slightly and she was glad to get back to her own chair where she could sit on her hands and hide behind the cool good manners of a hostess.

"Is there anything else I can get you?" She smiled serenely. "Why don't you stay and have some dinner here? Ali always cooks enough for at least three people, and I — and I'd like your company!" she ended with a rush.

"So you have been lonely!" he shot at her.

She swallowed, knowing that she was on the point of making a fool of herself.

"No, I haven't! But it's nice to hear someone talking English."

He laughed.

"*My* English? I'm afraid I speak it with a very bad accent."

It was impossible to tell him that there was no way that she would rather hear it spoken.

"It's still English!" she said flippantly.

He looked at her thoughtfully and she could feel herself flushing under his regard.

"Actually I came to talk about work," he said. "I'm taking a film out to a neighbouring village and I thought you might like to come along."

"Tonight?" she asked.

He nodded.

"It's quite a business setting up the screen and what have you. Also I think you will find it interesting. Will you come?" She hadn't realised how charming he could be when he wanted. Gone was that faintly irritable manner that he usually adopted and in its place an obvious desire to please that might have taken her in if she had been a little less wise.

"Are you making an outing for me?" she asked him abruptly. She didn't want to be in his way all evening merely because he thought she might be a trifle lonely!

He stood up, the smile completely gone and his eyes hard and searching.

"Certainly not!" he retorted. "I shall need your services tonight, Nurse. It is as simple as that. I shall pick you up here at seven-thirty." He cast one final glance in her direction and walked towards the door. "And wear something over your head to keep the sand out of your nose and throat."

"Wh-what sort of thing?" she stammered.

"You could do worse than buy a veil," he said dryly. "Ask Lala to help you choose one."

Of course he would like that! she thought angrily. Then he could laugh at her when she didn't know how to manipulate it properly. But at least *that* wouldn't happen, because if she did get Lala to help her buy one, she would also get her to show her how to wear one. She might even look very nice in it at that!

He arrived at twenty-five past seven on the dot, and one look at his uncompromising back as he brought the Land Rover to a screeching halt was quite enough to make her break into a run as she hurried over to join him. The back of the car was completely filled by the rolled-up screen and the projector with its massive batteries and loops of thick black wire. She stepped up into the front seat and sat down quickly.

"You're early!" she accused him, working on the principle that attack was the best form of defence.

"Four and a half minutes early," he agreed. "Did you get a veil?"

She nodded. She pulled it out and flung it around her shoulders and over her head, dragging one corner of it across her face. She rather liked the cool feel of the material against her skin, and she had to admit that Lala had taught her well, for it clung to her in easy folds and showed no signs of falling down the back of her neck, which had been her secret fear at first.

Dr. Kreistler regarded her critically.

"Very fetching!" he said at last.

She had enjoyed buying it too. Lala's enthusiasm had inspired the owner of the small general stores, and who had taken down his entire stock for the two girls to finger and try. In the end they had chosen a veil made half of wool and half of silk, a long length of white cloth that shimmered and glowed. It had been ridiculously cheap too, considering it was hand-made and embroidered all round the edges.

The sun was just setting as they drove out across the desert. The date-palms threw long, pencil-slim shadows across the sand that had a fragile beauty all their own, and the sand dunes looked dark and menacing, like enormous waves in the sea waiting to meet over their heads. Katherine shivered at the thought and closed her eyes so that she wouldn't see them. When she opened them again the whole sky was scarlet with great purple clouds gathering here and there in the distance. Then that too was gone, and the greyness of evening turned the whole world to monochrome that slowly deepened into the black of night.

The first sight they had of the village was myriad little fires, on each of which was probably balanced the inevitable tea-pot. When they came closer they could see the low black tents of the Bedouin and further away a clump of palms and a few houses.

A dozen children came tearing over the sand towards them.

"Bon soir!" they shouted, and the younger ones echoed: *"Bon soir, bon soir!"* without having the faintest idea of what it meant.

Dr. Kreistler stopped the Land Rover and within seconds a whole swarm of wriggling, excited young creatures had flung themselves on to it, hanging on to any purchase they could find and wildly adjuring him to drive like the wind. In fact he edged forward a few feet at a time, shouting at the top of his voice for them to get out of the way. But the children only laughed, and finally he was laughing too. Katherine hugged herself further into her new *haik* and began to enjoy herself. If the children weren't afraid of him, why should she be?

It took time to set up the equipment, and all the time a steady stream of people arrived over the dunes, whole families of them coming from miles around to see the doctor's films, their relations, and possibly even to arrange a suitable marriage for their sons and daughters while they were about it.

Katherine went and joined a large group of chattering women, drawing her veil closely around her, for now that it was dark it was getting cold. The women drew her nearer the fire and offered her tea, but Katherine refused their offer. From where she was sitting she could see the doctor talking to the head man of the village, and she thought how fine he looked and how well he got on with these people. Chantal would take him away from them. Chantal would never put up with the lonely silence of the desert and the constant battle against the sand. Chantal —

"Katherine!"

She started to her feet and hurried down the slight slope towards him.

"I'm here," she said.

He looked relieved to see her.

"I can't tell you from all the others in that blasted

haik!" he exclaimed impatiently. "I'm setting up an emergency clinic to deal with the nomads who have come in to see the films. I shall need you to help me sort them out." He turned on his heel and strode off towards one tent that was larger than all the rest. "Come on!" he said. "Hurry up!"

The sand got into her shoes and she stumbled once or twice as she desperately tried to keep up with him. Oh, botheration take the man! Why did he have to make her so nervous?

She had never seen anything like the inside of the tent. It was lined with highly-coloured silks, and rugs lay strewn across the sand. It was lit by powerful kerosene lamps that hissed and sometimes flared, sending ripples of shadow round the enclosed space.

Dr. Kreistler knelt on one of the carpets and opened up his bag.

"The rush will begin any minute now," he smiled at her. "The trick is to sort out the genuinely ill from the merely curious. Do you think you can do that?"

Katherine wasn't sure, but she was willing to try. She tried to imagine that she was helping a doctor at any ordinary clinic that she had ever attended, but she couldn't forget that he was *this* doctor and not just any other. Her fingers felt all thumbs and her few words of Arabic made nonsense, reducing the patients to silent paroxysms of mirth.

But somehow she found the ones who were truly ill and the ones who were only pretending, and managed to lance their boils and prepare the injections without dropping anything and thus disgracing herself entirely.

She was glad when it was all over and the right people had been given chits so that they would be recognised when they came to the hospital for further treatment and the others had gone away, proudly bearing their bandages and their medicines.

"You don't seem yourself tonight, Nurse," Dr. Kreistler told her as he snapped shut his bag. "Are you sickening for something?" He looked at her more closely, a worried frown between his eyes. "Have you been using the local water to clean your teeth in, or anything stupid like that?"

She glared at him angrily.

"I'm not a fool, Dr. Kreistler!" she told him proudly.

He grinned suddenly.

"No, I remember your saying so before. Ah well, if it isn't *that,* there must be something else the matter with you." And whistling softly under his breath, he ducked out through the door of the tent.

Katherine watched the films in a shaken silence. What on earth had he meant? Everyone had their off days when they didn't work as well as on others. And there was *nothing* the matter with her. Nothing, that is, except that extraordinary nervous feeling that he created within her, and that was no more than her natural dislike of being treated as a tiresome child!

It was an extraordinary experience, sitting on the sand in the moonlight, watching the films as they flickered on the enormous screen in front of her. All around her were the women, looking like so many sacks of potatoes as they sat in little groups, their veils held closely around them. The men mostly stood in pretended indifference, occasionally shouting a word of explanation to their women-folk, who sat too far away to hear the commentary properly.

Micky Mouse was a great success. Silence fell as they watched his antics with absorbed good humour. Then came the film on how trachoma was caused, with the doctor giving the commentary, sitting on the bonnet of his Land Rover, a microphone in one hand and a small boy clutching the other. The audience watched the little worms embedding themselves in

106

a piece of meat and followed their whole life history, seeing how they led to blindness in the person who ate them unless properly treated. It was a graphic lesson in hygiene, effectively and interestingly put across. Katherine was impressed, and she could well see why the government used this same method to explain the principles of democracy and local government to the nomadic tribes who wandered up and down the country.

It was late when it was all over. The screen was rolled up again and shoved into the back of the Land Rover together with the batteries and the projector and the other mysterious objects that were all part of the equipment.

Last of all the doctor came for Katherine and she walked beside him to the vehicle, smiling at the men who had come to see them off. She was completely unprepared, though, for him to lift her clear off her feet and into her seat. His eyes glinted in the starlight and she could see the white of his teeth. She sat, very upright, on the edge of the canvas and tried to pretend to herself that she felt exactly the same as she had before. This was a dangerous country, she thought, with its long silent stretches of sand and a moon and stars one could almost touch. It would pay her to guard her heart well or she would be lost.

He drove her right home to her door and he came round to her side and handed her down. For a moment she imagined she had felt his lips against her hair, and she wished that it had been so. She trembled slightly and the grip of his fingers on hers tightened.

"Cold?" he asked her.

But she couldn't answer him. Her throat was tight and it wouldn't allow the words to come.

"Stupid!" he said lovingly. "Go to bed. And don't forget to lock up well." He gave her a little push towards her door and she went obediently, drawing her *haik* closely about her. He was still watching her when she closed the door and rammed the great bolts home, but she couldn't see what he was thinking. She stood for a long moment with her back to the door and her heart hammering. She wasn't sure she could manage a charming Dr. Kreistler. An impatient one she had got used to, but this —!

It took her a long time to get to bed that night. The moonlight was beautiful behind the dark patterns of the palm-trees and the scent from the creepers in the courtyard was heady and full of promise.

"Stupid!" she repeated crossly to herself, but even then she couldn't hurry. It was a night that had been made for dreams and whispered longings, and it wasn't her fault if all her dreams were of the same thing. Tomorrow she would be sane again and Dr. Kreistler would be his old, impatient self and the world would be normal once more. And, with a sigh, she got into bed.

The morning brought a letter from Chantal with the information that she and her brother would be arriving at Sidi Behn Ahmed that very day and trusting that their rooms would be made ready for them. Katherine thought of her own arrival with a certain wry amusement, and told Ali to make up the beds in the other two bedrooms.

It was the first time she had ever had an opportunity of playing hostess in her own house, and she rather enjoyed herself, making sure that everything was in order, that there were towels in each of the rooms and a little bouquet of flowers in Chantal's. But once the preparations were over she began to wonder why they were coming and she knew that she was not looking forward to having the other girl arguing and sulking and planting her barbs. There wouldn't be much peace in the atmosphere then! But perhaps Dr. Kreistler would be pleased to see her.

She heard them coming from a great way off, the

dull roar of the engines echoing across the empty sand. They had come in two cars, the little mini-bus leading the way and Guillaume's drop-head coupé following close behind. Katherine went out to meet them, suddenly overjoyed to see Beshir's smiling face again. He sounded his klaxon in a triumphant solo and the two of them burst into laughter.

Chantal pressed her lips together and eased herself out of her seat on to the hot ground, her toes curling with distaste against her sandals. She looked, as always, immaculate, the creases down the legs of her trousers as sharply edged as ever.

"I had forgotten what a dump it is!" she said flatly, looking all round her. "If you have any pity you'll lead me straight to a long, cool drink and a shower."

Katherine laughed.

"I know just how you feel," she sympathised. "Sand in your mouth and sharp prickles of salt all down your back!"

Chantal remained unsmiling.

"You seem to have got very tanned," was all she said. "You look like a Bedu yourself."

Katherine turned away to greet Guillaume as he drew up behind the mini-bus. He didn't bother to open the door of the car, but stood on the seat and stepped over it.

"Katherine, my love," he greeted her, "aren't you glad we've come? Haven't you almost died with boredom down here all by yourself?"

"She hasn't been by herself," Chantal interposed coolly. "She has had Peter for company."

Was that why she had come? Katherine looked at her quickly.

"I can imagine it all," Chantal said evenly. "The two of you leading virtuous, solid, *dull* lives, working until you drop and then working again. Now that I have arrived it will all be different however."

Guillaume's quick eyes rested for an instant on Katherine's face.

"It's your fault that we came, you know," he whispered in her ear.

She looked up into his brilliantly blue eyes.

"Why did you come?" she asked him.

He shrugged his shoulders.

"What else did you expect us to do, without any money? We couldn't even entertain our friends properly on that pittance you allowed us. We came down here, like you did, to economise!"

Ali stood in the middle of the courtyard with a sullen expression on his face. He took a dab at a trail of sand that had blown in the doorway and drooped back again into his previous half-sitting, half-kneeling position.

"How long do they stay?" he asked Katherine.

Katherine shook her head.

"I don't know," she said repressively.

Ali hunched up his shoulders and looked more miserable than ever.

"Lala will not come while they are here," he informed her.

"Why ever not?"

He gave her a triumphant smile.

"Her husband will not allow it while you have a man staying in the house. All the women will stay away, and who will teach you Arabic then?"

Katherine sighed.

"I don't know," she said sadly.

She heard Chantal turn off the taps of the shower and a few seconds later the French girl appeared in the courtyard, languidly rubbing her hair.

"This place has become a hovel!" she announced. "The tap leaks, which is a shocking waste of water, and the plastic curtains are in shreds. How have you managed to put up with these things?"

Katherine forbore to tell her that all she had to do was turn the tap off harder. Instead she found herself apologising for the lack of amenities and wondered what on earth she was doing. *She* hadn't installed the plumbing!

Chantal gave her hair a final rub.

"I suppose I am in my usual room?" she said.

Katherine swallowed.

"You're in the room next to the kitchen," she told her.

There was an instant's silence, and then the French girl turned on the still kneeling Ali.

"You know I always have the same room!" she shouted at him. "Always! Always! Always! Go and change the beds at once!"

He looked at Katherine, his dislike for Chantal open on his face.

"Go and make some tea," Katherine told him calmly.

Chantal stamped her foot, her slipper making a slapping noise against the polished tiles.

"I will not sleep in that horrid, poky little room!" she stormed. "The other is cooler and bigger."

"But unfortunately already occupied," Katherine said calmly.

Chantal opened her mouth, thought better of it, and shut it again. She went to the bedroom Katherine had given to her, opened the door and slammed it shut after her. In a few seconds she opened it again.

"You'll regret this!" she said hoarsely. "Uncle Edouard may have left everything to you, but he didn't intend this!" And the door slammed again.

Katherine sat down heavily on one of the wicker chairs and buried her face in her hands. The de Hallets had arrived with a vengeance! When she looked up, Guillaume was there, his blue eyes mocking her.

"You're silly to take her on," he said simply.

111

"You'll never win in the long run because you haven't the heart for the battle."

"It's *my* room now!" Katherine retorted. "Why should she have it?"

"Why indeed?" he agreed. "But it wasn't the room I was talking about."

Katherine gave him an impatient glance, and was glad when Ali brought the tea. She poured out the golden liquid with trembling hands and handed Guillaume the lemon and the sugar.

Of one thing she was quite determined. Chantal could do what she liked at Hammamet, but down here it would be different. It was *her* house and she would run it exactly as she pleased, and she didn't give a *damn* what Uncle Edouard had intended!

CHAPTER EIGHT

CHANTAL spent most of her time sunbathing. She would lie full-length in the middle of the courtyard, dressed in nothing more than a bikini, and let the sun turn her to the colour of mahogany. Ali pretended at first that he couldn't see her and refused to bring her anything at all from the kitchen until she was fully clad. But, later, he became quite concerned about her.

"She will become silly from so much sun," he said to Katherine. "Someone should tell the doctor and then he will stop her, yes?"

Katherine was not bluffed by this anonymous someone; she knew it would have to be her. And yet she shrank from the task. Somehow it seemed a little like bearing tales, and who wanted to be accused of that? In the end she decided to say something to the other girl herself.

"You shouldn't sit in the sun so much," she began quite mildly. "It could make you very ill."

Chantal gave her a languid look from her pale blue eyes.

"And what else do you suggest I do in this God-forsaken hole?" she asked.

Katherine tried to picture her doing any of the hundred and one things that she had found to do and failed dismally. Chantal had been in the country for years, but she still couldn't speak a word of Arabic, and showing the women how to bath their babies properly and how to nurse them when they were ill would undoubtedly bore her to distraction.

"Why did you come?" she asked her lamely.

Chantal looked amused.

"You're so innocent, my dear," she retorted. "Peter

is all man, and in your undiluted society he might even fancy himself to be getting fond of you." She surveyed herself complacently. "What's the matter? Don't you like the competition?" she grinned suddenly, in an almost likeable way. "It is pretty hot, isn't it?" she said.

"Very hot!" Katherine agreed dryly. "But you needn't have worried. I've hardly seen Dr. Kreistler at all. A few moments here and a few moments there, but no more than that."

Chantal studied her hands, fussing over a broken nail. It was funny how the dryness all around made it almost impossible to keep one's nails all in one piece.

"Ah, but," she drawled, "those few moments became so important, didn't they? The highlight of every day!" She looked up suddenly and her eyes were bright and hard. "I am not a complete fool, *Nurse* Lane."

Katherine bit her lip, horribly aware of her hot cheeks as she remembered the drive home through the desert after the film show. But then she hadn't been denying that the moments had been important to her. It was *him* that Chantal was concerned about.

"I think you underrate your own powers of attraction," she said, and felt very close to tears. She couldn't even be amused by Chantal's obvious and complete agreement with this statement. Somehow that hurt more than anything else, not because of Chantal at all, but because she was very nearly sure that Dr. Peter Kreistler would have agreed with her. How could there be any comparison when the French girl was always chic and beautifully groomed and she herself was no more than a lost child with dust on her eyelashes?

It didn't make matters any better when the first person she saw at the hospital was the doctor himself.

"Got a minute, Katherine?" he called to her.

He wasn't very smart himself, really. He wore a shirt that had once been blue, but the sun and constant washing had long since changed it to a pale shade of grey. And his sand-coloured trousers were nothing to write home about either. It was the way he wore them that gave them that air of being better than anyone else's.

At the moment he was frowning, his strongly marked eyebrows meeting in impatient displeasure. Katherine's heart sank within her as she searched her conscience for something she had left undone, but there was nothing that she could call to mind. Nothing at all.

"Is something the matter?" she asked him quietly.

"What's all this about your turning Chantal out of her bedroom?" he barked at her. "Surely the house is big enough for the three of you to live in it in peace?"

Her head went up proudly.

"Quite big enough," she said stiffly.

"Well then?" he demanded.

"It's *my* house!" she said crossly. "And how I run it is my own affair. If Chantal doesn't like it, she can go back to Hammamet."

His long, level look made her nervous. She was angry too, furiously angry that Chantal should have been to him because for once she hadn't had her own way, and just a little bit angry because he had weighed in so willingly on the French girl's behalf.

"Did you turn her out of her bedroom?" he asked at last.

"I don't see that it's any of your business!"

He put a hand on each of her shoulders and forced her to look at him.

"I'm making it my business! Did you?"

She held out for as long as she could, glowering up at him, hating him because he was so concerned. Then her eyes fell and she said:

"I didn't see why she should have it. I had been sleeping there ever since I came."

He let her go abruptly, and she stumbled backwards from him until she was leaning against the surgical green wall of the corridor.

"Did it matter so much?" he asked. He sounded indescribably weary of the whole business.

She supposed that it had been rather childish, and yet she had had to draw the line somewhere, or else she might just as well have handed everything over to Chantal and gone back to England. Only it was impossible to explain such a thing. It wasn't logical, it was just something one felt.

"I had to show her it's my house," she said, and thought how terribly inadequate she sounded. If it had been Chantal, she wouldn't have had to show anyone anything. It just would have been so.

To her surprise the doctor smiled at her.

"I see," he said, and then added: "Don't let these possessions of yours go to your head, will you? There are other things in the world." He ran a finger down the side of her cheek as he had done once before. "It doesn't suit you to throw your weight about," he said cheerfully, and, whistling a surprised little tune under his breath, he strode off down the corridor towards the maternity ward.

Katherine stood there, looking after him. Chantal was more fortunate than she knew, she thought, to have such a man fighting her battles for her.

Guillaume's car became a familiar sight to the people of the oasis. They hardly bothered to look up now as he flashed past them, and even the children lost interest in the bored, restless man who seldom stopped to talk to them. Katherine fell into the way of going with him whenever she had nothing else to do. She never grew tired of looking at the ever-changing, ever-the-same qualities of the desert

116

all around them; the grey-yellow of the sand and the bright green splashes of the oases. Others might long for cooler skies and soft green fields, but Katherine was quite content with the harsher scenery all around her.

Guillaume, on the other hand, hated everything about it. Sometimes she would find herself worrying about Guillaume. It seemed terrible to her that he should have nothing to do — no wonder the man was bored! She even found herself giving up her other occupations to go with him, and as Dr. Kreistler made no comment about it — indeed she doubted whether he had even noticed! — she didn't feel badly about not attending so many clinics with him. There were other nurses, after all. She wouldn't admit, even to herself, that what she wanted was for *him* to insist that she accompanied him, that anything would have been better than his calm indifference as to what she did.

"Why don't you go back to France and manage your own estates?" she asked Guillaume one afternoon, as he set the car down one of the lesser known tracks going south, deeper into the desert.

He laughed a trifle bitterly.

"And desert Chantal?" he asked. "She is my sister. I couldn't leave her in Tunisia on her own. One day, when she marries, who knows?" He shrugged his shoulders fatalistically. "She is older than I am, and I have always done what she says," he ended comically.

"Perhaps it would be better for her if you hadn't!" Katherine couldn't resist saying.

"Perhaps," he agreed. "We are neither of us very nice people, you know. But I, at least, have my moments of compunction." He looked at her earnestly until she wished he wouldn't as the car slewed almost off the track. "Don't take Chantal's threats too lightly," he warned her. "She wants the Hammamet property for herself and somehow she will get it. It is nothing personal, you understand. It is simply that she already considers it hers, and you are the usurper."

As if she didn't know that! But she didn't like to say it was that very impersonality that she found so frightening, for there was nothing she could do to change it.

"And you?" she asked him. "Do you think of me as a usurper too?"

He smiled and his blue eyes were very bright.

"I think of you as a very lovely girl, what else?" he said. "And lovely girls are my specialty. I never do anything to hurt them."

Katherine stirred uneasily beside him. She had the uncomfortable feeling that Guillaume must have hurt a number of women in his time and that he considered them fair game when it came to kissing and running. How odd that she had never thought about him in that light before.

She began to tell him how she had seen them fertilising the date-trees by hand that morning, for the best dates were far too valuable for such an operation to be left to chance, and anyway, who knew what pollen might blow across to them from the more indifferent trees? She had admired the skill of the workers as they climbed the long bare trunks and had made the locals laugh when she had been concerned for their safety. As a change of conversation it wasn't very successful. She might have known that Guillaume wasn't in the least interested in dates and wasn't to be so easily distracted.

"You ought to have something better to do than gazing at the natives," he told her slyly. "I'm sure that's not at all what Uncle Edouard intended when he left you everything."

Katherine gave him a sharp look and wondered

why this continual harping on Edouard de Hallet's intentions should make her so cross.

"I don't see how you, or Chantal, or anyone else for that matter, could possibly know what he intended!" she said shortly.

He slewed the car off the narrow road and brought it to a stop.

"My dear Kathy," he said, "I should have thought it was obvious! One glance at all that luscious hair of yours and I knew *exactly* what he had intended!"

"Did you?" Her voice was icy. "You must have been alone, then, for everyone else seemed to find it as much of a mystery as I do."

He reached out a casual hand and tried to pull her into his arms, but she eluded him.

"Don't you want me to kiss you?" he asked her. He sounded hurt, like a rebuffed child, and his eyes were bluer than ever.

"No."

He laughed, and she knew that his conceit would never allow him to believe her. She was annoyed with herself for getting into such a situation and even more annoyed with him for being so obtuse.

"I expect you'll like it all right when it comes to it," he informed her loftily. "I've never known a girl struggle too hard when it came to it!"

"If there were as many as all that," she retorted bitterly, "I don't suppose you even remember their names, let alone whether they liked your attentions or not!"

For some extraordinary reason he seemed flattered by that.

"At least I shan't forget your name," he promised her.

She began to wonder whether it wouldn't be simpler to let him have his way. She had been kissed before, and although she hadn't enjoyed the experience very much, she hadn't objected either. But she didn't want to be kissed by Guillaume. It wasn't that she disliked him, it was just that she felt he was the kind to kiss and tell! Tell whom? Her cheeks became hot at the thought, and she hurriedly opened the car door and slid out into the hot loose sand on the edge of the track.

Perhaps it was fortunate that at the same time she heard the first beats of a nearby drummer, followed by the wailing welcome of some women. She had watched them often, putting a finger in their mouths and running it round their lips as they made that wild, weird cry.

"It's a party!" she exclaimed to Guillaume, and set off rapidly across the sand in the direction of the noise.

He followed her without hurrying, his camera slung over one shoulder and a slight smile on his lips. Oh dear, she thought, wasn't he even now going to take no for an answer?

She crossed another rise of sandstone, standing gaunt and yellow against the lighter shade of the prevailing sand and saw the little collection of houses beyond, dazzlingly white in the hot sunshine. An old man had picked up the rhythm of the drums on his flute and the dancing had already begun. Katherine ran towards them, joining a little group of women on the outskirts whose brightly-coloured clothing had caught her eye from the top of the ridge.

"What are you celebrating?" she asked them.

They moved over to allow her to see the dancers, but they were too shy to answer her questions. She clung to their company, however, for she didn't think Guillaume would press his advantage by following her over to them.

She watched him as he lit a cigarette, looking down at the colourful scene from the top of the ridge.

"This won't amuse you for long," he called out to her. "It's only a local wedding."

"I've never seen one before," she called back.

He came slowly down the slope, undoing the case of his camera as he went.

"There's nothing to see. The groom will be at the nearest mosque with his friends and they won't let you see the bride."

"Why not?" she asked him.

He grinned at her.

"You might put the evil eye on her. Come on back to the car."

She was disappointed. She wished she had brought her own camera to take some photographs of the dancers and of the women in their spectacular dresses and *haiks*.

"Will you wish the bride good luck from me?" she said to the nearest of them. It was difficult to make herself understood, but at last the message was understood and a little crow of approval went round the group.

"Come," they called to her. "Come."

She hesitated, turning to Guillaume, silently seeking his approval. With a shrug of resignation, he seated himself on the ground and smiled up at her. Really, she thought, as she turned away, he wasn't as bad as he liked to make out. And perhaps he didn't really mean to kiss her. Perhaps it was only that he thought all girls expected some kind of flirtation under similar circumstances. He was still watching her as she followed the women into the closely guarded compound, and she gave him a little wave of her hand to show she had forgiven him. The de Hallets were bewildering people to be with. One never knew where one was with them from one moment to the next.

It was terribly hot in the compound. The woven grass fencing cut out all the breeze and there was nothing but the hot sand and the metal-coloured sky that brooded over it. Wave after wave of feminine hands pushed Katherine to the centre of the excited crowd of women who had packed themselves into the enclosure, and at last she reached the centre where the bride sat, closely veiled, in the brand-new clothes that her husband-to-be had brought her. Katherine recognised immediately the satin quilted basket that lay, discarded, beside her, and the five-branched decorated candles that had been carefully put beside it.

The bride's mother smiled a greeting and made room for her to sit down in the closely knit little circle of relatives and friends who sat round the bride, and the silence that had greeted her presence was broken and the babble of chatter broke out again all around her.

It took the bride longer to lose her shyness, but after a little while she loosened her veil and finally threw it right back from her face, her curiosity getting the better of her modesty. She looked very young, but proud and mature in the way that she smiled at Katherine. There was a little heap of some kind of corn in front of her, and she reached out for a handful and let it trickle out on to the top of her head.

The heat became greater every moment and Katherine began to wonder if she could bear it. She accepted a small sweetmeat and ate it very slowly, hoping the dizziness would wear off. It wasn't very sensible to sit with the sun directly behind one's head, and she longed for a cooler shadow and something behind her back to lean on.

When she could bear it no longer, she rose to her feet and smiled all round. The bride giggled and stood up too, following right to the doorway of the compound, all thought of the men outside forgotten. Her mother came after her, screaming instructions at the top of her voice, pushing and shoving her way through the other women. But she was too late. In the instant that the girl had stood there, her face quite naked to the people outside, Guillaume had lifted his camera and had snapped her.

"I've got her!" he shouted, well delighted. "Run, damn you, or we shall have the whole village after us!"

But Katherine could only stand there, as dismayed and as angry as everyone else. How could he have done it? For even he knew that no good Muslim woman would ever allow anyone to take her photograph.

"I am sorry," she said to the angry men. But they completely ignored her. It was Guillaume they wanted, Guillaume and his camera.

She stood watching with a sense of fatalism as they overtook him and brought him, struggling, back to the compound. An older man, who could only have been the bride's father, wrenched the camera from him and stamped on it. Guillaume went white in the face.

"Have you any idea what that camera's worth?" he demanded. "I'll sue you for this!"

The bride's father regarded him with contemptuous eyes.

"Why do you wish to bring my daughter bad luck?" he asked. "Why do you wish to take an image of her for other men to stare at? So that her husband will divorce her before they are even wed?"

Katherine took one look at Guillaume's stubborn face and bent down to retrieve the camera. It wasn't badly damaged and she thought it could quite easily be repaired. With trembling fingers, she opened it and took out the film, silently handing it to the Berber.

He took it quite gently from her, exposing its long length to the rays of the sun.

"The insult still remains," he said almost calmly. "The man stays here."

She stared back at him in an appalled silence.

"But —" she began.

"The man stays here!" There was a finality in the man's tone that brooked no defiance.

"We'll have to run for it," Guillaume said, without looking at her. "Run for the car and I'll follow when I can."

She hated leaving him, much as she condemned what he had done. It was so silly to ride rough-shod over other people's customs and beliefs, but who would persuade a de Hallet of that?

She took to her heels and ran up the sandstone in a single rush, arriving breathless at the top. The car stood reassuringly where they had left it, the chromium glinting like glass in the sunlight.

"Happy landings!" Katherine wished herself. That at least still had the power to amuse her, though she couldn't remember who it was who had first brought the saying to the hospital where she had trained. For years it had been a part of her life, mingled with exams and patients and operations. It had been a talisman of a kind and it had brought her luck.

She reached the car and got in it, sitting on the burning hot scarlet leather with a little *ouch!* of surprise. She looked over her shoulder and saw that Guillaume had succeeded in following her. She reached over and opened his door for him, and then sat back and left the rest to him.

She was furious that she had ever come with him. The story would soon spread through all the nearby oases. It would be common gossip in every market place for miles around and, more particularly, in the market place of Sidi Behn Ahmed where she was known and liked, and there it would undoubtedly reach the ears of Dr. Kreistler. She flinched away from the thought, almost hearing his stinging comments before he had even uttered them.

Guillaume swung the car round and headed back down the rough track towards home, leaving a group of angry Berbers standing on the roadside shaking their fists at the fast vanishing car. It had all been so unnecessary, upsetting them in this way, and who would blame them if they took their revenge if they could?

It was a painful and silent journey home. To Katherine it seemed quite endless. The sun beat down on her and she felt dizzy and peculiar. The only thing to do, she thought, was to go straight to the hospital and tell Dr. Kreistler herself. She couldn't allow *his* work to be compromised in any way.

They were almost at her house when Guillaume started to laugh.

"What's so funny?" she asked him sourly.

"The whole affair! Would you have believed that people could behave like that? She wasn't even particularly pretty!"

"That wasn't quite the point," Katherine said shortly.

"Wasn't it?" He laughed again.

"No, it was not. And I hate to think what the repercussions will be. Dr. Kreistler will be furious with us both!"

"And you care?" he drawled.

She jumped out of the car and faced him, angry from the top of her head to the soles of her feet.

"Yes, I care!" she told him fiercely.

It wasn't quite so easy to face Dr. Kreistler himself. She could tell by looking at him that he had had a long, hard day, and his impatience, never very well hidden, always frightened her a little.

"What do you want?" he demanded when she ran him to earth in his office at the hospital.

She stood there in silence, not knowing how to begin.

"Well?"

She started, stopped and sneezed instead.

125

"I can't tell you anything when you look so cross!" she complained.

He laughed and his eyes became very kind.

"Can't you? It usually pays to begin with the worst, I've heard. Nothing seems quite so bad after that, you see."

She felt herself relaxing a little and she even managed a rather tired smile to show him that she appreciated his thoughtfulness.

"Guillaume took a photograph of a bride, unveiled," she burst out without adornment. "Her father was furious and he wanted to keep Guillaume there, but we escaped and drove straight home."

His look of distaste was something she could hardly bear.

"And where was this?" he asked.

She explained to him as well as she could, her voice ashamed.

"I gave the father the roll of film, but he wasn't satisfied with that," she ended.

"It wasn't your fault," he said consolingly. "Though I could quite cheerfully strangle Guillaume de Hallet! I'll go out myself this evening and sort it all out."

She was afraid of crying, and she swallowed hard and then quite unmistakably sniffed. He offered her his handkerchief and watched her with a professional eye as she mopped herself up.

"I don't suppose you want to tell me why you stopped at that particular corner of the road?" he remarked, and watched the colour fly up into her cheeks. "No, I thought not," he went on conversationally.

"Guillaume finds it so boring down here," she cut him off defensively.

"And you?"

She was genuinely astonished that he should ask.

"I love it," she replied simply.

He smiled, holding out his hand for his handkerchief.

"I thought as much. If you take my advice you'd encourage young de Hallet to go back to Hammamet."

"And Chantal too?" She could scarcely hide her eagerness, and was a little shocked by her own inability to hide her dislike for the other girl.

But Dr. Kreistler only laughed.

"Chantal is harmless enough," he said.

She wanted to tell him that she was probably the more harmful of the two, the more spiteful and the more vindictive, but the words died on her lips. He took both her hands in his and pulled her into the circle of his arms.

"You have a quaint, helpless look with your hair done up like that," he told her.

She screwed up her nose and blinked as she looked up at him. Privately she thought his features stood up very well to this close scrutiny. She liked the warm brown of his skin and the firmness of his mouth.

"And when it's down?" she asked breathlessly.

He gave her a light kiss on the forehead and released her.

"Why, then you look like a princess out of a fairytale!" he teased her lightly.

"Peter!"

They both swung round, and Katherine's heart went cold within her, for standing in the doorway was Chantal, looking lovely in one of the smartest dresses she had ever seen.

"Hello, Chantal, my dear," the doctor greeted her calmly enough. "What brings you to the hospital?"

The French girl laughed without any amusement at all.

"I thought I'd come and find out what kept you so busy over here," she said sweetly. "What *else* keeps you so busy, I mean!" Her eyes swept round the office and rested for an instant on Katherine, and then dismissed her.

"Are you going to show me round?" she asked.

CHAPTER NINE

KATHERINE was sitting under the date-palm in the courtyard when Chantal came back from the hospital. The last of the evening sun had changed the glaring white of the walls to a softer hue and the bright blue paint of the doors and the windows had become a vivid purple. It was in many ways the best time of the day, when it was cool enough to do all the things it had been too hot to do all day, and the time when all the little birds in their cages began to sing and when the perfume of the flowers was at its heaviest.

In contrast Chantal looked hot and tired. The dry air was not being very kind to her skin and little lines were beginning to gather at the corners of her mouth and between her eyes. If she was not very careful, Katherine decided, they would set, stamping her face with the permanent marks of spiteful bad temper. She wished she hadn't noticed them because she knew that she would always see them in the future, and in a curious way they added to her dislike of the other girl.

"What did you think of the hospital?" she asked her quietly.

Chantal smiled briefly with secret amusement.

"To be honest I hardly glanced at it," she admitted. "I haven't your enthusiasm for the smell of antiseptic. And that terrible green paint! Where did they dig that up?"

Katherine giggled involuntarily.

"Perhaps they thought it would match the green of the surgical overalls," she suggested. "I rather like it. It looks so clean."

"Exactly!" Chantal agreed with feeling. "And

talking of cleanliness, have you seen my clean night-dress anywhere?"

Katherine blushed slightly.

"Ali put it in my room," she admitted. "You have some lovely things," she added without rancour. "I think Ali thought so too, judging by the careful way he spread it out on the bed!"

Chantal looked distinctly put out.

"I suppose he thought it was too good for me!" she said nastily. "Haven't you any pretties of your own?"

Katherine shook her head, a little amused.

"Nothing *quite* like that!" she said dryly. And just as well too, she told herself with robust common sense. Her fair and rather average looks would be completely swamped by such magnificence. "I'll give it to you when I go upstairs. Shall I put it in your room?"

Chantal gave her a long, enigmatic look.

"No," she said at last. "I shall fetch it myself."

She walked slowly up the stairs, her shoulders drooping a little. Katherine watched her go, wondering why she should worry about the other girl, who was really more than capable of looking after herself. She hadn't had the reception she had expected from Dr. Kreistler, that much was obvious, and yet Katherine thought that he would have welcomed her interest in his work. Perhaps he was one of those men who liked to separate his work from his pleasure, and yet — oh, how very much she would have liked to know what he really thought about the de Hallets and about herself!

She sat on in the darkening courtyard, half dreaming and half wondering if she hadn't put too much store on building the canning plant at Hammamet. It was so terribly difficult to know whether she was doing the right thing. She didn't want to be unfair to the de Hallets, but on the other hand, there must have been some reason why Edouard had left the properties to her, and what could it be if it were not to conserve them and improve them and make them a paying part of the new Tunisia?

She heard Guillaume's car roar into the market square and didn't even look up as he came through the archway of the door. He came and stood over her, looking down at her until she felt self-conscious and opened her eyes and looked back at him. Immediately the colour flooded up her cheeks and her eyes opened wide, for it was not Guillaume at all but the doctor.

"I thought it was Guillaume's car outside," she said.

"It was," he replied briefly.

"Then —"

He smiled down at her.

"Do you mind if I sit down?" he asked her.

She shook her head and he sat down opposite her, watching her closely under his dark bushy eyebrows. Katherine became horribly aware of her creased dress and the traces of sand on her face that she had forgotten to wash off. She didn't compare very favourably with the chic Chantal, she thought, and took refuge in gazing down at her hands so that she needn't look at him.

"You don't seem very hospitable this evening," he remarked in amused tones. "Aren't you going to offer me a drink?"

Her eyes flew up to meet his and dropped again.

"I'm sorry," she murmured. "I didn't think you'd be coming in tonight. Have — have you been out to the wedding village?"

His face hardened and she wished she hadn't brought the subject up.

"Yes, I went," he said. "I made Guillaume drive me out there, as a matter of fact." He was silent for a moment, then he said quite gently: "There's no need to look like that, my dear. No one blamed you for the incident. Even the villagers were quite clear about that."

"Did Guillaume apologise to them?"

"Not exactly, but he made them very handsome reparation, and they were quite satisfied with that."

She stood up and went into the kitchen, returning with a whisky and soda which she handed to him with a smile.

"Thank you for sorting it all out," she said.

He accepted the drink and sipped it thoughtfully.

"I hesitate to ask it of you," he said, "but you could prove your gratitude by not going on these expeditions with Guillaume in the future."

She sat down again, drawing her feet up beneath her.

"I don't suppose he'll be so silly again. I think he gets bored and lonely down here with nothing to do."

"I shouldn't be surprised," the doctor said dryly. "But don't feel that you have to entertain him. He isn't at all clear-headed about his future at the moment."

"Are you forbidding me to go out with him?" she asked, bewildered.

His lips twitched and she thought with a little rush how *nice* he was despite his rather impatient manner.

"Have I really that right?" he asked her.

It came as rather a surprise to her to think that she had ever considered that he had.

"Of course not!" she denied quickly. "But was that what you meant, all the same?"

He smiled, looking a little guilty.

"Yes, it was," he admitted. "The de Hallets are going through a bad patch, and I don't think this is a good time to get too involved with them."

Katherine stiffened involuntarily.

"You mean not all right for me but all right for you!" she exclaimed heatedly.

He looked surprised.

"I think you are reading too much into this. I meant it as a friendly warning, no more than that."

"Indeed?" She felt flustered and rather indignant, and the memory of Chantal's inopportune arrival at the hospital and her own dismissal from the scene still burned within her.

The doctor nodded, still looking more than a little amused.

"Why not? It is pleasant for you to have an escort, of course. When you first arrived down here you worked much too hard. You needed some relaxation."

"I was happy!" she retorted.

His glance softened.

"Were you? Nevertheless I think I should have done more for your entertainment. I shall make up for it now by asking you to accompany me for dinner to an ex-patient of mine. It will be good for you to see an Arab household like this one, but unfortunately the track to his house is too bad for a car. We should have to go by camel. Will you come?"

Katherine hesitated. Out of the corner of her eye she could see the skirt of Chantal's dress hovering at the top of the stairs, and she wondered irritably why the other girl didn't either come down and join them or go right away.

"I should love to," she said at last, and saw the skirt move back and then come forward again as Chantal began to come downstairs.

"Am I invited also, *chéri?*" the French girl asked the doctor prettily.

He stood up, his eyes widening slightly with appreciation at the picture she made, standing among the exotic blooms of the creepers.

"I think not, my dear," he replied gently. "It is not quite your sort of outing."

Chantal descended the stairs in a rush, pouting at him.

"But if you will take Katherine —"

He laughed.

"Katherine I can see on a camel — you, I cannot!" he said, and he made it sound like a compliment. Certainly Chantal took it as such, for she gave him a very gracious smile and seated herself on the arm of his chair.

"Perhaps you are right," she said softly. "There are other times for you and me to go out together."

The doctor gave a noncommittal shrug of his shoulders and drained his drink.

"I must go," he said. "I shall pick you up at six o'clock tomorrow evening, Katherine?"

Katherine nodded her head, not looking at him. For her much of the pleasure of the outing had been taken away. Chantal was so very sure of herself, and so very sure that she had Dr. Peter Kreistler in her pocket, that it was difficult not to believe it.

"I shall be ready," she said.

He smiled at her, right into her eyes, and she was comforted.

"Wear a dress with a wide skirt," he instructed her. "Goodnight!"

He walked out without a backward glance, leaving the two girls together. Chantal slid easily into the chair he had just vacated, her pale blue eyes never leaving Katherine's face.

"Don't be too clever, my dear, will you?" she said silkily. "I am prepared to accept your taking the legacy that was due to me, but I should not accept your taking my man also."

Katherine held her head high and took a deep breath.

"*Is* he your man?" she asked quietly.

Chantal's colour rose angrily and the little lines round her mouth showed more plainly than ever.

"I have told you so. That should be enough!" she said grandly. "But if you really need convincing, why don't you ask him?" And Katherine was shocked to see the real dislike that shone out of her eyes. She was pretty safe there, she thought, for she was far too frightened of the doctor to ask him anything of the sort.

Katherine dressed with care the following evening. She chose a frock of pale blue dressed cotton that had a wide, flared skirt and a neat fitting bodice that suited her well and accentuated the fairness of her hair. With it she wore blue leather sandals and long black gloves that matched her handbag and some black ebony beads that had been given to her as a child.

There was no sign of either Guillaume or Chantal as she made her way downstairs and out into the market square to await the doctor, and she couldn't help feeling rather relieved that they wouldn't be there to witness the first time that she mounted a camel. To tell the truth she was a little afraid of the great, haughty animals that the Arabs treated with such a casual respect, and she couldn't imagine herself riding one with any ease or grace at all. But it was too late to cry off now, and anyway she was anxious to see this house that Dr. Kreistler had wanted to take her to. She wouldn't admit, even to herself, that it was the idea of an evening in his company that was so attractive.

He arrived on the dot of six, with two camels accompanied by their laughing owners, who thought the whole occasion was a great joke. The animals looked very tall to Katherine and quite unbearably disdainful.

"You look very nice!" the doctor greeted her.

She brushed down the skirt of her dress, secretly pleased that he should think so.

"I have to admit I'm terrified of your camels," she said.

"Are you?" He looked surprised, as though it hadn't occurred to him that she might have any doubts about riding any kind of animal. "It's very easy really. The secret is to lean back and not cling on to the front of the saddle."

The saddle! That for a start was a misnomer! It was no more than a framework of wood lashed together with string and covered by a couple of brightly-coloured striped blankets. The doctor grinned at her and signalled to one of the camel-boys to make his beast kneel down. The camel groaned, swore vigorously and started on the perilous descent to a kneeling position. With another groan it subsided completely on to the dusty ground. It didn't look nearly so overbearing when one could look down at it, and Katherine felt distinctly better about the whole thing.

Dr. Kreistler helped her to settle herself on her perch of blankets just behind the single hump, and the great beast started laboriously to rise, the back legs first and then, with a frightening lurch, the front ones also, staggering a little to regain its balance. Then he jumped on his own camel and led off the strange little procession, out of the dusty market square and along the narrow, windowless streets of the village. The children came running out to see them pass, calling out greetings as they ran alongside.

"Where do you go?" they asked. "Why do you go there?" And lastly: "Is it a marriage? Can we come too?"

The doctor answered them all with a cheerful good humour, hurrying his camel forward, though that reluctant beast refused to break out from the plodding walk that came more naturally to it.

Katherine became used to the jolting motion quite quickly and began to enjoy herself. From her high seat she could see over the hedges that surrounded the oasis allotments, catching glimpses of the neat rows of vegetables and the occasional pink or white of blossom. The date-palms grew tall and straight and a few bananas fought for space beneath them, seeking their share of the sun and the carefully controlled water. She still found it rather startling to see all this vigorous growth in the middle of the harsh dryness of the sandstone terrain.

It was fully an hour before they came to the end of the narrow track and found themselves once again among dry yellow cliffs that were strangely reminiscent of the scenery of a Western film. They travelled upwards and then dropped down again into a little basket of green away from the main springs of the oasis. Already Katherine could hear the drums of the band and the swirl of their home-made bagpipes.

"There's the house," Dr. Kreistler told her, pointing towards the edge of the green of the palms. "It doesn't seem possible, does it? To build such a place so far from anywhere?"

Truly the house could have come straight out of the Arabian Nights. Its domes towered upwards towards the sky, miraculously white and smelling slightly of dry distemper, an unromantic touch that somehow made the whole thing seem more real, for even the soft playing of the fountains and the brilliant colours of the massed flowers looked more as though they had come out of a dream than that they were a part of reality. Katherine was glad that she had taken the trouble to dress up, though nothing short of a full-length evening dress would really do such a place justice.

The camel-boys began to urge their gangly-legged beasts forward, uttering shrill cries of encouragement as they ran forward a few feet and pulled on the short rope that was their only contact with their charges. The camels plodded slowly on regardless, completely ignoring their young masters' efforts. And then, quite suddenly, they were there, and the camels were reluctantly collapsing again to allow them to dismount.

Katherine stood rather shakily and smoothed down her dress, making sure that she was not dishevelled by the long ride. Dr. Kreistler came over and joined her, looking critically down at her.

"Will I do?" she asked him. "Do I need some more lipstick?"

He took her hand in his, smiling slightly at her nervousness.

"You look very nice," he said. "Come and meet your host."

They walked slowly through the gardens towards the noise of the band and the sound of laughter and, rounding the corner of the house, they came across a group of Arabs, some of them in European dress and others in their national costume, watching the dancing display that their host had put on for them. One of them, a tall man in a burnous and sandals, came towards them and shook them both by the hand.

"Welcome to my house," he said formally. "Everything that I have is yours."

Dr. Kreistler returned the formalities in fluent Arabic and then turned back to Katherine.

"May I introduce Selim Behn Ahmed El Badis, Miss Katherine Lane."

The Arab bowed low over her hand.

"I am honoured that you should adorn my house," he said easily. "Now that you are here we shall eat, and then we can watch the dancing again when the night is cooler and we can enjoy it better." He led the way to the table that had been placed on one of the spacious verandahs. "Will you sit one on either side of myself?" he asked them.

Katherine caught a glimpse of the women of the

household behind a latticed screen, and felt suddenly shy at finding herself alone in this completely male party.

"Could I not join your wife and daughters?" she asked him.

Selim gave her a look of approving indulgence and regretfully shook his head.

"It would not be practicable. They speak no French at all, like all the women of Tunisia, but they will be delighted when I tell them that you asked to join them. Perhaps later I will take you to meet my wife." He pulled out a chair for her to sit on and she sat down hastily, hoping that she had not put Dr. Kreistler in a difficult position by her suggestion. She could feel his eyes on her face, unblinking and watchful, but she had no way of knowing what he was thinking. She cast him a quick, shy smile and was relieved when an answering gleam came into his eyes and he looked away from her and began to talk to his next-door neighbour.

The meal was strange but delicious. Selim himself served her from the great bowls of food that were brought round by the veiled women, explaining gently how she should eat each item and what it was called.

"This is *brik,*" he said, pointing to a brittle envelope of crust in which was folded an egg together with some herbs. "It is eaten with the hands, like this."

She tried to follow his example and thought she managed pretty well, though there was some laughter at her efforts.

"You like my country, do you not?" he asked her suddenly.

"Oh *yes!* Very much!"

He gave a little nod of satisfaction.

"That is well. Edouard de Hallet was a wise man, and I can see that he did well when he left Sidi

Behn Ahmed to you. There is much that needs doing to the land in the new Tunisia, and we cannot afford to be greedy in what we take out of it. The de Hallets have never learned this, I think. I am pleased that I can welcome you as a neighbour."

Katherine flushed with pleasure.

"But I know so little about the management of property," she said. "Sometimes I'm afraid I shall do the wrong thing. It's so difficult to know always which is the best thing to do."

He nodded sympathetically.

"And you have the de Hallets with you? That also must make difficulties." He finished his *brik* with a little flourish of his fingers. "I shall tell you an old fable of Tunisia. Will you listen?"

Smiling, she nodded her head.

"It is the story of a little gazelle from the steppes," he told her. "A graceful, charming little animal as fair in colouring as yourself. She became very thirsty, as you can imagine, in the hot sun that beat down on the dry land, so she thought that she would go to a little grove of palm-trees that she knew about where there was a small amount of water. But on the way she met a fox who was also very thirsty, though he had done nothing to make him so, and this fox asked her whether she knew of all the dangers that could meet her in the palm-grove, saying that it was better that he should go on first and protect her, for he knew that there was only sufficient water for one of them.

"So the fox ran on ahead, but when he reached the water the mocking-bird mocked him and the watersnake kept him out of the pool, while the other animals snapped and snarled at him from behind the cactus bushes. And Monsieur Fox — or Madame Fox — had to withdraw, and when the gazelle came to the pool it was all safely waiting for her to drink. So you see that grace and gentleness are far stronger weapons than cunning in the desert steppes where the palms grow wild!"

Katherine laughed.

"It's a charming story," she agreed. "I hope I am the charming gazelle and not the cunning fox!"

Selim smiled slowly.

"I think we can safely say that you are," he said. "Don't you agree with me, Dr. Kreistler? Would you not protect her drinking water?"

It wasn't a fair question, and yet Katherine found herself waiting breathless for his answer. For if she was the gazelle, who was the fox?

"Yes, I should," the doctor replied. "But I think she is already aware of that, aren't you?"

His bright eyes caught at her heartstrings, relentlessly demanding something of her. What a time to start flirting with her, she thought indignantly, but she liked it all the same. She liked the warm tan of his skin and his thick, bushy eyebrows, and she liked the way his hair grew out of his scalp. Oh yes, he certainly knew how to make her aware of his charms.

"I don't know," she said demurely. "Sometimes I think so."

Selim smiled delightedly.

"You are slipping, *mon ami*," he said to the doctor. "If Miss Lane were my girl she would be quite sure!"

The doctor laughed.

"I am sure she would," he agreed smoothly.

Really it was an impossible conversation! Katherine looked indignantly from one to the other of the two men, but they only smiled back at her, both with a faintly indulgent air that she thought she ought to dislike but actually found rather flattering. It was rather nice to pretend, even for one evening, that she was Dr. Kreistler's girl. It gave her a warm, comfortable feeling, and she hoped that he, on his part, was not minding too much. But it seemed that he was not, for he smiled straight at her and said firmly:

"Don't look so worried, darling, I really will keep the foxes away — the wolves too, come to that!"

She blushed despite herself and was glad when the women came to take away the plates and brought in the next dish, the traditional meal of North Africa, the *couscous*. It arrived in an enormous pottery dish covered by a grass-woven lid. It was a rich, very hot mutton stew, resting on steamed grains of millet — a dish that could be rich and expensive or cheap enough to suit the pocket of the poorest peasant. Katherine enjoyed it, and she enjoyed listening to the men talk about the local affairs, about how much easier it was not to persuade the people to attend the local clinics and the new and better prices that were being received by the villagers for their dates.

The evening seemed to pass by in a dream of talk and dancing and a mixture of the weird, complicated rhythms of the Arabic music and the simpler if no less stirring music of the Negro players.

It was late when they started back for home. The camel-boys talked idly between themselves, occasionally shouting a word of encouragement to the slow, plodding animals in their charge. Katherine urged hers forward, closer to the doctor. The barren hills all around were as black as ink and the moon hung low in the sky with little trails of silver cloud all round it. But mostly it was the incredible silence that made them seem so alone in the world, as if they were the only man and woman left in the world apart from the two chattering boys who did their best to ignore them.

"Selim is nice," she said sleepily. "Is he really so very rich?"

"It's difficult to tell. He owns about thirty thousand date-palms, and that means big money around here."

Katherine yawned. She was pleasantly tired in a way that she could enjoy, and she was making the most of it.

"I wonder how many date-palms I own," she said.

Dr. Kreistler was amused.

"Don't you know?" he asked.

She shook her head.

"Every time I get a little bit of knowledge in my head something else comes along and I'm back where I started. It was all so much easier when I was nothing more than an ordinary nurse. I think I was happier too in a way."

He reached out a hand and squeezed one of hers.

"You will be again," he whispered to her. "I can promise you that!"

And she would have believed him if Chantal hadn't been waiting up for them.

"You look exhausted, Katherine!" she greeted her, with a quick breathless laugh. "Go upstairs to bed and recover from that dreadful animal and I'll give the doctor a nightcap."

Katherine glanced at Dr. Kreistler and he nodded to her.

"Yes," he said, "go on to bed, my dear. You are already half asleep. I shall see you in the morning?"

She wanted to thank him properly for taking her out, but she couldn't with Chantal there, listening to every word, and so she only smiled and started up the stairs.

"Peter darling," she heard Chantal whisper behind her, "I thought you were never coming, and you *promised* that you wouldn't be late and that you would take me for a walk in the moonlight."

Kate gained the landing and slipped off her shoes from her aching feet. She did, after all, feel quite abominably tired and very, very much alone. She got quickly into bed and turned out the light. There were other things to think about besides the moonlight, and she would be wise if she turned her attention to them. Tomorrow she would go and call on Lala and have another Arabic lesson, and she would also find out exactly how many date-palms she really possessed. And that would be a start at least towards being a successful landowner, for if she couldn't compete with Chantal in any other field at least she knew she could do better in that one! And she badly needed something to boost her confidence.

CHAPTER TEN

CHANTAL came in late. Katherine heard her creep up the stairs and enter her room, and a little while later she heard her light go out and knew that the other girl had settled down to sleep. She, on the other hand, lay awake, restless and dissatisfied. The moon had long since disappeared over the edge of the horizon and the night was so black as to be frightening. It was silent too. Uncannily silent, without even a bird uttering, or even a camel spitting bad-temperedly at its mate.

Had Chantal locked the front door? The thought occurred to her with devastating suddenness and then she couldn't get it out of her mind. She could picture someone out there pushing it quietly open and coming into the house. Don't be silly, she told herself. What if they did? No one around here would want to hurt her or either of the de Hallets, would they? But it was no good, she would have to go down and see.

With a sigh she reached for her slippers and drew her gown over her shoulders. The cool night air was soft against her face as she padded down the stairs into the courtyard beneath, and she saw that not only had the door not been locked — it hadn't even been closed. With a gesture of impatience she went towards it, and at the same instant a shape moved in the shadows. She froze to the spot where she stood, listening for the slightest sound, but all she could hear was her own uneven breathing.

"It's all right. It's me," the doctor's voice said quietly beside her.

And quite suddenly she was furiously angry.

"Haven't you gone home yet?" she demanded.

"If you must moon over Chantal, why don't you go and do it somewhere else?"

She could hear the gasp of his laughter.

"Why? Does it bother you?" he asked her.

"Of course not!" she denied crossly. "But I want to get some sleep tonight, if you don't!"

"Ah, but how do you know that I was hanging after Chantal?"

She began to wish that she had put her dressing-gown on properly so that she didn't have to hold it tightly together at the throat.

"I should have thought it was obvious!" she retorted. "Walking for hours together in the moonlight!"

He came very close to her and drew her into the circle of his arms.

"For a nurse," he said softly in her ear, "you are very given to jumping to conclusions."

Her knees felt weak, and she could feel her heart shaking within her.

"I believe the evidence of my own eyes!" she said tautly.

But he only laughed again, and he was so close that she could feel his breath against her hair.

"Let me go!" she demanded urgently. But his arms only closed more tightly around her and, despite herself, she could feel herself giving in to their pressure. In another moment, she thought, he would kiss her, and then she would be lost. He would know then exactly how she felt about him and it would be too late to pretend.

"Dr. Kreistler, will you please go so that I can lock up after you?" She had meant to sound firm, and was dismayed by the distinct note of pleading that had entered her voice. "Please, Peter!" she said more urgently.

His arms fell away from her.

"Perhaps you're right," he agreed gently. "There

will be other times. Goodnight, my dear, sleep well."

When he had gone she wanted to call him back. But she couldn't do that. He had proved that he really did belong to Chantal and that was that. Other girls had had to cope with similar situations. There was nothing new about it, nothing to burst into tears about, so why was she crying? There were other men in the world besides Dr. Peter Kreistler — but there was none with quite the same indefinable charm and none who could stir her to the very depths of her being by saying her name in just that way. But then he was the only Hungarian she had ever known. If she did but know it they probably all said it in exactly the same way.

She bolted the doors with automatic fingers and was almost surprised to find that she had done so. There was nothing now to keep her downstairs, and yet she couldn't bear to go back to bed.

It was funny really. She had left Hammamet because she had disliked living in the same house as Chantal, and yet how infinitely preferable that had been to having the French girl and the doctor together. That was something that she would have to grow used to, but she couldn't stay to watch the affair blossom into love and marriage. Oh no, she would become a landowner in earnest and make pots of money. She would go back to Hammamet and begin her apprenticeship under Brahim, and later — a long time later — she would come to Sidi Behn Ahmed and learn all about dates too!

But she couldn't help wishing that she had allowed Peter to kiss her just that once. It wouldn't have meant anything to him, but she would have had it to remember all her life.

It seemed like fate the next morning when there was a letter waiting for her from Brahim. Guillaume

147

tossed it down on to her side-plate at the breakfast table and made a face at her.

"More worries, Kathy?" he suggested.

She tore open the envelope and took out the single sheet of coloured paper within.

"Don't call me Kathy," she said automatically.

"Why not? It's a pretty name."

Katherine shrugged her shoulders impatiently, a gesture that she had caught from the doctor.

"Very pretty, but it doesn't happen to be my name," she said sweetly.

Guillaume looked at her closely, his blue eyes very bright.

"You've changed since you came to Tunisia," he said abruptly, and it was obvious from his tone that he didn't think it was a change for the better.

"Perhaps you're just getting to know me better," Katherine suggested indifferently.

"Perhaps," he agreed. "But I don't think so. I think your dislike for Chantal and myself has hardened into a more positive thing. Is that it?"

Katherine hesitated, loath to hurt him.

"I think it's just that we're not each other's kind of people," she said gently. "I don't dislike you, Guillaume. I don't feel anything very much either way."

He blenched.

"Well, you could hardly be more devastating than that!" he said with a self-mocking laugh. "I hadn't supposed I was quite so colourless."

Katherine was horrified.

"But you're not!" she insisted. "It's just that no man really shows to advantage when he hasn't anything to do. Does he?"

He smiled at her, his eyes sad.

"You are right as always. I shall go back to France before it is too late and marry a nice French girl who will think I am wonderful. Is that what you want?"

She nodded.

"That's what I want," she said.

"And Chantal?" he asked her.

Katherine's eyes dropped back to her letter.

"Chantal will be marrying herself," she said lightly. "You worry about her too much."

"So it is she whom you really dislike," he said with some humour. "Ah well, I suppose I cannot blame you for that. Chantal is not an easy person to love."

It sounded worse, somehow, put into words. She didn't like Chantal, in fact she actively disliked her, but she didn't altogether like to admit the fact. To stop herself thinking about it she turned back to her letter.

"There's salt in one of the water supplies feeding the orchards," she announced fatalistically. "Guillaume, do you think I ought to go up to Hammamet and see for myself?"

His eyebrows shot upwards.

"Running away?"

She nodded bleakly.

"Very well," he said, "there's no need to ask. I'll get us a couple of tickets on the railway and we'll run away together. You to Hammamet and me to France."

And in that moment she came nearer to liking him than she ever had done before.

Chantal didn't come down until lunchtime. With a sinuous movement she sank into a chair and smiled with a superior air at no one in particular.

"Peter has promised to take us all to Tozeur tonight," she announced in pleased tones. "We'll all dress up and make whoopee, yes?" She turned to

Katherine. "I suppose you have an evening dress?" she asked in bored tones.

"Yes, thank you," Katherine replied gently. She didn't want to go. But oh yes, she did! She would give anything to have the opportunity of dancing with Dr. Kreistler! She wanted that!

"Isn't it rather a long way to go for a dance?" she asked.

Chantal shrugged.

"Peter knows how dull it is down here for me. Naturally he wants to keep me reasonably entertained. Otherwise he knows I'll go back to Tunis and the bright lights, or even Hammamet."

Not Hammamet, please! Katherine prayed silently but fervently. Anywhere else, but not on top of her, not any longer!

She still couldn't quite believe that they would really go so far until she actually got into the car, squashed in beside Chantal, who naturally sat right in close next to Dr. Kreistler, from where she could whisper to him, just under her breath, in the most irritating manner. Really, Katherine thought, perhaps she had changed, for little things like that had never been able to disturb her patience so easily before. She refused to admit that it was because these particular little things concerned the doctor. It would be unwise to admit to a thing like that even to oneself.

The white salt of the Chott Djerid seemed endless. In daylight the glare was intolerable and after dark it was weird and rather frightening. Katherine began to wish that she had cried off the expedition. But she couldn't have done that. Guillaume would buy their tickets as soon as they got to Tozeur and tomorrow she would be starting back to Hammamet. She flushed a little in the darkness as she remembered Dr. Kreistler's amused surprise at the amount of luggage she had taken with her for an evening's entertainment. If he had only known the suitcase contained practically everything she possessed!

Chantal was still talking in soft, intimate whispers when they arrived at the outskirts of the oasis. Katherine turned round to Guillaume, who was sitting perched on one of the seats behind.

"Are you very stiff?" she asked him sympathetically.

"Not too bad," he answered her. "How are you?"

The doctor grinned at him in the driving mirror.

"Don't ask her!" he said. "We'll all change round on the return journey and Katherine and I'll share your perch. What d'you say, Nurse?"

There wouldn't be any return journey! Katherine opened her mouth to stammer out some such thing, but Chantal's cool voice cut across her chaotic explanations.

"Katherine wouldn't feel safe with you," she said in a lingering note of intimacy. "Didn't you know she was afraid of you?"

The doctor leaned right across her.

"Are you, Katherine?" he asked.

Her eyes met his and fell away again.

"Yes, I think I am — a little." She caught her breath. "How ridiculous! No, of course I'm not afraid of you. I don't understand you very well, that's all it is."

"That is easily remedied," he said gently.

Her fingers moved uneasily in her lap and her mouth felt dry.

"But I'm not sure I want it remedied," she said at last.

She could almost feel Chantal's triumph, as though it were a living tangible thing beside her.

"There! What did I tell you?" the French girl exclaimed. "You see! You will have to content yourself with teasing me this evening, Peter. I can take it, for I understand you only too well, *mon cher!*"

"Quite so," he replied smoothly, his voice completely devoid of all expression, "but where there is no mystery there can also be no fascination, don't you think?"

Katherine's startled glance met his, but there was no mercy in his eyes, no tenderness. Did he know? Was it possible that he knew how she felt? But no, that was ridiculous! She hardly knew how she felt herself.

"Never mind," she heard him say, and all that customary impatience was back in his voice. "What does it matter? We came to dance, nothing more."

But she felt that she had disappointed him all the same. But she wasn't the kind who could flirt lightly and pass on her way. How she wished she was!

The hotel was floodlit, the yellow bricks standing out sharply against the deep black shadows that accentuated their patterning. Katherine looked for the boys who had been selling their dates and sandals in the entrance the last time she had come, but they had gone home for the evening. There was only one older man with a collection of postcards right inside the hotel, and he didn't have the same glamour of his daytime counterparts.

"Shall we eat straight away?" Dr. Kreistler asked the party amiably.

"Must we? So soon?" Chantal pouted.

Katherine looked urgently at Guillaume and he smiled at her reassuringly.

"In half an hour," he suggested easily. "I have one or two things that I must do, but then I shall be entirely at your disposal."

Dr. Kreistler looked from one to the other of them and his mouth tightened ominously.

"And you, my gazelle," he said to Katherine, "what do you want?"

She didn't feel very like a gazelle that evening.

The gazelle had got the water through her charm and grace and she felt only devious and cunning. She ought to tell the doctor that she was going back to Hammamet.

"Half an hour will suit me very nicely," she said.

"Then you can come and dance with me meanwhile," he said masterfully, and led her willy-nilly into the bar where some of the residents had rolled back the rugs from the floor and were amusing themselves dancing in time to some music from the wireless.

"What about Chantal?" she asked breathlessly. Her feet felt like lead and the music was strange to her. Besides, she was frightened of Chantal. She had been all along, ever since the French girl had dropped the phial of perfume she had given her on the pavement. Remembering it, she shivered slightly, and the doctor's arms tightened angrily about her.

"Am I so very unattractive to you that you cannot bear me to touch you?" he asked her bitterly.

She stumbled against him, and it was a second before she recovered herself.

"Well?" he demanded.

"It was a goose walking over my grave," she said in a shaken voice.

He gave her an exasperated glance.

"You say you do not understand me, but it is I who do not understand you!" he said angrily.

She blinked, hoping that she was not going to cry.

"It's an expression," she explained laboriously.

"An easy expression that means nothing! So handy to turn away the inquiries of a stranger, is that not so?"

She looked at him wearily.

"Perhaps," she said. "I don't know."

His face softened unbelievably, and her tears spilled over and rolled slowly down her cheeks.

"It isn't you! It isn't you at all!" She looked up at him bravely, letting him see her tears. "I'm going back to Hammamet," she said baldly. "And Guillaume is going back to France. He's tired of having nothing to do. I can understand that, can't you? He's really very nice. I like him." She was talking too much, she thought, and she stopped abruptly, wishing she had never begun.

"Yes, my sweet, I like him. And I think it is a good thing for you to go back to Hammamet. When do you leave?"

"Tomorrow."

So he didn't care at all. Naturally he thought it was a good idea for her to go away. He would be free of the responsibility for her then and he could concentrate all his attentions on Chantal — and she hated them both!

"We're going up by train tomorrow — *together!* So you have no need to worry about my traipsing about the country without an escort."

He smiled.

"That seems a very long time ago," he said.

She sniffed.

"You weren't very kind," she told him.

His eyebrows flew up and his eyes were full of gentleness.

"Wasn't I? I thought I was very reasonable."

She spluttered into laughter.

"You don't know what it means to be reasonable! But don't change!" Her fingers tightened against his arm. "Don't ever change!"

He stopped dancing and looked down at her with the utmost seriousness.

"I rather think that rests in other hands than my own," he said.

Chantal's hands? They wouldn't leave him to work himself to death in an obscure oasis in North Africa. He would end up in Harley Street, or whatever the equivalent was in Paris, with his hair all smoothed down and a kindly bedside manner, and she wouldn't like him one bit.

"I wish you luck anyway," she said bleakly. "I hope you get your heart's desire."

And she wondered why he smiled in quite that way.

"I haven't entirely despaired," he told her.

Katherine slipped out of the circle of his arms and glanced towards Chantal, who was sitting at the bar, sipping a drink with stony-faced indifference.

"Hadn't you better dance with Chantal?" she suggested. "I'll go and see if the management can find rooms for Guillaume and me tonight."

"Very well," he agreed. He lowered his head until his lips were on the same level as her ear. "But I choose my own partners. Remember that!"

She watched him go across to Chantal and seat himself on one of the tall stools beside her, ordering himself a drink. He looked handsome in his white evening jacket and black tie. It was funny, but she had never thought of him as being handsome before. It was his strength she had got to know, and his great love for all kinds and conditions of men. And his caustic impatience, *that* she had come to love. Yes, to love! And why not? She wasn't ashamed of it.

She felt Chantal watching her and shivered again. She threw her a brief smile and turned away quickly. Guillaume would be back with the tickets soon and they would all want to eat, and before that, she had to make her own arrangements with the hotel. She couldn't expect Guillaume to do everything; she owed him enough for being so willing to escort her back to Hammamet.

They could hear the beat of drums and the thin

wail of the first experimental flute searching for a melody as they sat down to dinner.

"Oh, are they going to play?" Katherine asked eagerly.

Dr. Kreistler smiled at her.

"Only incidentally. They're coming to provide background music for the snake charmer. He's bringing his creatures in to show the visitors later on."

Chantal looked pleased.

"I love snakes," she announced calmly. "They fascinate me. They look so wicked and spiteful and devil-may-care!"

"And are really quite ordinary beings," the doctor put in, "looking for a warm place and a quiet life."

Katherine gave him a swift look of gratitude. She had never known any snakes intimately and as far as she knew she didn't want to. She was terrified of all creepy-crawlies and she always had been.

"That's true," Guillaume smiled. "They are far more frightened of us than we are of them!"

Katherine was more than half convinced they were right when she saw the *fakir* who was going to show them the snakes. He was tall with a chubby face and a cheerful, half-embarrassed laugh that rang round the room at regular intervals. He dressed to the part, wearing enormous baggy camel-trousers and *djellabah* that showed the signs of many a wash and long hours out in the desert. On his head he had tied a large cloth and had tucked the edges in behind his ears without too much success.

"Does he really charm snakes?" Katherine asked.

The men shook their heads.

"He has a very fine collection, though," they insisted. And truth to tell she was rather glad. She thought it added to rather than detracted from his charm that his snakes didn't do all the usual things. She would far rather see them, if she had to, being themselves.

156

She wasn't quite so sure when he started to produce them, casually, out of the carpet bag that he slung over one shoulder.

"A viper!"

There were several high-pitched gasps from the women who watched him and a nervous giggle from a Chinese gentleman who was something to do with the United Nations.

The *fakir* slowly circled the room, going from person to person to show them the forked tongue and the soft, dry skin of the long, wriggling snake.

"You like it?" he asked Katherine.

She forced herself to look at it, but no, she didn't like it! She felt cold with horror inside and could feel the colour draining out of her cheeks.

"Perhaps you prefer scorpions?" he laughed down at her. "I have many scorpions."

"Perhaps I do," she agreed readily, quite willing to say anything to make him take the snake away. Chantal pressed her hand against her arm.

"Why, I believe you are afraid of it!" she taunted in her sly, cool voice. "We can't have that, can we, Guillaume? Tell him to bring out his scorpions next. They're the cutest little things!"

The *fakir* dropped the viper on the polished floor and captured it neatly with a forked stick, dropping it back into its bag.

"Oh, let me see!" Chantal exclaimed. "Have you got another stick like that one! I should so love one! Look, Peter, he's actually gone to the trouble of polishing it!" She wrenched it out of the Arab's hand and sat down again, triumphantly waving it over her head. "May I have it? Please, may I have it?"

The *fakir* nodded, a little reluctantly, Katherine thought, and she felt rather sorry for him for having his hand forced like that. Her distaste for Chantal flared up again within her and she moved her chair surreptitiously a couple of inches away from her,

157

then wished she hadn't, for in doing so she had moved backwards as well, and in her lower chair she couldn't see anything but the French girl in front of her.

The Arab slowly and impressively re-tucked in the ends of his headgear and bent down and opened a large wooden box he had with him. Out of it he produced a couple of small jars and spilled the contents out on to the floor. Two scorpions, completely different in size and colouring, faced each other and started curling up their venomous tails. The *fakir* separated them with the toe of his sandal and the larger of the two started laboriously to crawl towards Chantal's chair.

The French girl watched it with horror in her eyes for a few seconds and then she waved the stick at it.

"Take it away from me!" she screamed. "Take it away!"

The Arab smiled and started towards it, but Chantal was quicker. She reached out with the forked stick and flicked it upwards straight on to Katherine's lap.

Katherine froze. She knew it was the only thing to do. The beast was already sufficiently frightened to sting anything with which it came in contact, and all she could do was to give it very little opportunity to sting her. It was Peter Kreistler who removed it. He took it away in a cloth and returned it to the angry and now sullen *fakir*.

"It was her fault!" the Arab said furiously. "Why did she do this thing? Does she hate so much she must kill?"

Katherine gasped and she turned swiftly to Chantal. What a terrible accusation to make! But the other girl was now quite cool again. Her pale blue eyes met Katherine's inquiringly and then she smiled enigmatically.

"Were you very frightened?" she asked curiously.

Katherine felt suddenly calm and more relaxed than she had done all day.

"Not very," she said slowly. "Were you? It could have been a nasty incident."

Chantal stood up leisurely and smiled again.

"But not an accident, darling," she drawled softly, and with a light laugh, made her way towards the bar.

Dr. Kreistler brought the Land Rover to the front of the hotel and opened the door for Chantal to get into the front seat. Katherine stood on the concrete step to the hotel and raised her hand in farewell. Her head was aching and her knees felt weak and decidedly wobbly. It was funny really, she had thought that her heart would break when it finally came to the time when she had to say goodbye to the doctor, and all she could feel was an overriding sense of relief that he was taking Chantal away.

He came up to her, his shoes crunching on the loose chips on the road. He put up a hand and touched her cheek gently with his firm, capable fingers.

"Look after yourself, my dear," he said.

"I will!"

He smiled at her.

"I hate to see a good nurse go, but I think you will be safer at Hammamet."

"Far safer," she agreed.

"So you think it was deliberate," he said thoughtfully. He shrugged his shoulders with an impatient movement. "I'll see you when I come north?"

She nodded. She couldn't do more. All she could think was that he was glad to be rid of her rather than to think anything unpleasant about Chantal. But then he hadn't heard her say it hadn't been an accident, so how could he possibly know?

The Land Rover moved forward and was soon lost in the enveloping darkness.

CHAPTER ELEVEN

GUILLAUME looked remarkably cheerful in the morning. Now that he had made up his mind to go back to France he was a different person, and a much more likeable one.

"The train leaves in half an hour," he warned her. "Do you think you can be ready?" His blue eyes twinkled outrageously at her. "I know what women are!" he went on. "Never on time! Always in a hurry!"

"Nurses are always on time," she retorted. "They have to be."

Guillaume shook his head sorrowfully.

"Nurses are the worst of all. In their private lives they are always late. I have noticed this fact often. Perhaps it is because they have to be on their toes all the time in the hospitals."

A glint came into Katherine's eyes.

"Half an hour, did you say? I'll be there, waiting on the platform. But will you be? You haven't shaved yet!"

He felt his rough cheeks with an offended air.

"A *nice* girl wouldn't have noticed," he rebuked her.

Katherine smiled and stood up, leaving her napkin in a heap on the edge of the breakfast table.

"Perhaps not," she agreed dryly. She might not have noticed either if the sun had not been shining right in across his face. He was so fair that his beard was scarcely noticeable — not at all like Peter Kreistler, whose lopsided face with its bushy eyebrows was altogether more definite.

Guillaume stood up too.

"Now, now," he said gently. "Don't *brood!*"

Katherine made a quick little apology and started on her way up to her room, but she couldn't help wondering whether Guillaume knew that his sister's action had been quite deliberate. She hadn't tried to kill her exactly, but she certainly wouldn't have been sorry if she had come to any harm. They were queer people, these de Hallets, with their bitter selfishness and their cruel ways. Even Edouard had expected to be treated differently from anyone else she had ever nursed, but she had managed to like him all the same. It was only Chantal that she both feared and disliked — and it wasn't any easier because she was also jealous of her and she had never known jealousy before, nothing like this blinding, scorching emotion that left her feeling both empty and unattractive.

She packed away her night things with trembling hands and went down to the hotel entrance to wait for Guillaume. He came, hurrying, with odd bits of his clothing creeping out of his suitcase and his raincoat tossed over one shoulder.

"We'll just make it!" He grinned across at her. "Just as well too, for these trains only leave twice a week."

"Oh, come on!" she said impatiently. She had a sudden, awful fear that they really would miss the train and that she would have to go back to Sidi Behn Ahmed.

But the train was still waiting at the small terminus. It was a long collection of open wagons with the single passenger carriage stuck on at the end almost like an afterthought. Most of the open wagons were empty, waiting for their heavy loads of phosphates that they would pick up at Gafsa and carry laboriously northwards to Sfax and Tunis.

Guillaume produced their tickets and they climbed aboard the old-fashioned carriage on to the open verandah at the back. The guard carried their luggage into one of the compartments and accepted his tip with a calm dignity.

"We leave in two minutes, sir," he said respectfully.

And rather to everyone's surprise they did leave exactly on the hour appointed and began the long haul north.

It was a long and tedious journey, passing first through the phosphate belt and then through the endless steppe-lands towards Sfax and the miles and miles of olives. El Djem, the third biggest Roman arena in the world, caused some excitement as they went past, but otherwise there was very little to see that was new to them. At another time Katherine would have enjoyed the experience, but in her present numbed state, nothing seemed very important, and she had quite enough to do, trying to keep reasonably cheerful for Guillaume's sake.

It was a matter of relief all round when they finally arrived at Hammamet and were able to shake the dust out of their clothes and wash their hands and faces that had been covered by a film of grey dust from the loading of the phosphates.

Feeling a good deal fresher and more normal, Katherine stepped out of the station and waited for Guillaume to find a taxi. A few seconds later they were heading through the small town and out towards the fruit estate. The green of the trees and the strong, vivid colours of the masses of flowers were strange to her eye after her weeks in the south. Even the wild flowers seemed exotic and almost as though there were too many of them.

They came to the wrought-iron gates of her own house, and Katherine gazed at the long drive, lined with trees, with a new pleasure. The perfection of the house and grounds no longer overawed her. She was glad to be there now that she knew that Chantal was somewhere else. It felt like home.

It was lonely at first when Guillaume had left for Tunis as the first stage of his journey to France. Katherine went from room to room and planned the few small changes she would make in their furnishings, trying to pretend to herself that she hadn't already reached the first stages of boredom. There was nothing whatever for her to do in the house; there was a large and very capable staff that took care of all the housework and the cooking. Respectfully, once a day, they would ask her to approve the menus, and then everything would go on as before with clockwork perfection.

On the third day Brahim came up to the house. Katherine saw his tall, patriarchal figure from the window and went running down the drive to greet him. He salaamed magnificently from his great height, and she felt she ought to curtsey or do something equally formal in response, but in fact she offered him her hand and left it at that.

"I came to greet you home," he said gravely.

"How nice of you," Katherine responded warmly. "I was worried by the salt you said was getting into the water."

He looked at her solemnly, saying nothing. Katherine flushed slightly.

"There were one or two other reasons as well," she found herself confessing, "but that was the most urgent."

"Of course," he agreed gently. "Will you come and see the orchard concerned now?"

Katherine nodded eagerly, pleased to be doing something positive, and they set off through the gardens towards the enormous orchards beyond.

"How's the money going?" Katherine asked. "I want to be able to tell Monsieur Verdon when I see him that we have at least been able to make a start."

Brahim looked far into the distance, his face calm and undisturbed.

"We shall start building next year if all goes well," he said calmly.

Katherine's eyes shone with excitement.

"Really? But that's wonderful! How have we managed so quickly?"

He smiled at last, transforming his whole face into a mass of happy wrinkles.

"One can only spend money once," he said reasonably. "A few prudent economies and it begins to add up in the bank. Young Monsieur de Hallet wrote to me and told me he would have no further need for his allowance. This was a good thing. We only have the one drain on our resources now, and that too will not last for ever."

No, Katherine thought with surprised displeasure, she couldn't see Dr. Kreistler accepting money from anyone on behalf of his wife. She would have to live on his income or do without. She wondered briefly how Chantal would like that, and felt a certain grim amusement as she pictured her reaction. She doubted if Peter would give her many nightdresses like the one Ali had so admired. Peter was essentially practical and he would expect his wife to show the same sense of proportion. She gave a little giggle, and Brahim looked at her inquiringly.

"It was nothing," she said hastily. "Just a thought."

An answering gleam of humour came into his eyes.

"It is ever so with women," he said, totally without patronage. "The sense of the ridiculous is ever with them. With my wives, I no longer ask what it is that amuses them."

She laughed, uncertain as to whether she had been thoroughly snubbed or not.

"Your wives?" she asked at last, rather uncertainly.

It was his turn to laugh.

"I have two wives," he said quietly. "It is no longer legal to marry two women, but I have been married many years to both my wives."

"And are they good friends?" she couldn't resist asking.

He laughed again.

"Of course! On these occasions it is the man you must feel sorry for. Most women have a very good understanding, one with another!"

Katherine chuckled, liking him more than ever.

"I should like to meet them one day," she said, "when I know a little more Arabic."

Brahim nodded.

"They will be honoured." He walked briskly through one of the gates that opened in the earth walls that divided one orchard from another. It was a sad sight that met their eyes. The fruit stood out on the bare branches of the trees, a few to each branch, small and withered. Brahim picked up a couple of the fallen leaves in his hand and rubbed them between his palms. "Salt," he said, "is our big enemy in this country."

Katherine looked at the devastation around her and sighed.

"What can we do about it?" she asked helplessly.

"We shall have to close the spring," Brahim replied. "There is some reason why it should suddenly become saline. Perhaps some other stream has crossed its path. We do not know. We must dig and find out, or maybe we must call in the experts so that they can tell us."

"I see," Katherine murmured. "Will it be very expensive?"

Brahim did some calculations on his fingers.

"A little expensive," he said at last.

Katherine hadn't known that the water-supply was obtained from springs, and she said so now.

"Oh yes," Brahim told her. "There are many thousands of springs all around here. That is what Hamma means in Arabic — a spring. You will find the same name at El Hamma. In fact there are two El Hammas." He went on to outline his plans in greater detail, making quick little drawings in the dust to illustrate his explanations.

"You know a great deal about irrigation," Katherine said admiringly.

He nodded gravely.

"I am an excellent manager," he agreed seriously. "If I had not been the best Monsieur de Hallet would never have employed me." He stood upright abruptly and started to walk back to the house. "It will be fine if everything is left in my hands," he added, suddenly suspicious of her interest.

"As it will be," she assured him. But she was sorry, all the same. He didn't really need her help at all. In fact she knew that she would only be in the way, preventing him from doing more important things, if she insisted on his explaining every detail of the management of the estate. "I have so very little to do up here that I'm bound to be interested, though," she went on humbly.

He gave her a look that might have been sympathy and went on walking.

"Dr. Kreistler will come north soon," he said gruffly. "Waiting always makes the hours seem long."

Katherine stared at his retreating back, her indignation boiling up within her. Did he really think that? Could it possibly be true?

"But Dr. Kreistler is nothing to me!" she said out loud.

His face crinkled up in that sudden way it had.

"What woman will ever admit it?" he said simply.

They parted company on the edge of the pleasure gardens and Katherine went on to the house alone. The dying fruit-trees depressed her, or so she told herself. It was time she got about and met some people, she decided, and thought about something else besides herself and her own problems. Accordingly she rang up the Verdons and told them she had returned to Hammamet. Madame, who answered the telephone, was delighted.

"My dear, you must come and see us immediately," she cried. "Can you bear the muddle our house is in? We are re-distempering the outside and we are doing a great deal of it ourselves to save costs."

"What fun!" Katherine said immediately. "Can I help?"

There was an instant's hesitation from the other end.

"But of course, my dear, if you really *want* to?"

"I do," Katherine assured her. "There's nothing for me to do in my own house, and I'm not used to an idle life. Can I come now?"

She heard Madame's surprised and pleased laugh quite clearly, followed by a very French squawk as she thought of something else.

"Is Chantal with you?" she asked.

Katherine licked her lips. Was this it? Had Chantal been right when she had said that she would never be accepted without the French girl's backing?

"No," she said hoarsely.

"Good!" Madame laughed brightly. "I do not wish to be unkind, you understand, but when one has Chantal to one's house one must be all dressed up and everything must be just so. With you it is different, I think?"

"Very different!" Katherine agreed in relieved tones. "How do I get to you?"

Madame Verdon's instructions were brief and to the point, and Katherine had no difficulty in finding the right house. It was much smaller than her own and very French to look at, with shutters at every window and a large painted wooden door that stood wide open in a perpetual welcome.

The Verdons were both perched on the top of

step-ladders with a large bucket of distemper in one hand and a brush in the other.

"Hasn't it a horrible smell?" Madame greeted her cheerfully.

Katherine looked up at her and grinned.

"Revolting," she agreed.

Madame put her bucket down on the top step and came slowly down the ladder, holding out both hands to her guest at the bottom.

"You are thinner!" she announced frankly. "What have you been doing with yourself? Come inside at once and I shall make coffee and you will tell me all about it, *hein?* No, it is no trouble at all. I have been working all day and I need a short rest."

She led the way through the pleasant house to the kitchen where she made coffee without any fuss and clucked anxiously over Katherine.

"I am angry with myself!" she told her crossly. "Peter rang up two nights ago and asked me to make sure you were all right, but I have been so busy here, and I kept telling myself that another day wouldn't hurt. And now that I see you, I can well understand his anxiety!"

"I am a little thinner," Katherine admitted, "but surely I don't look so badly. I'm very well and quite a lot browner."

Madame poured the coffee into two large, pottery cups.

"You look tired — and scared," she said flatly. "And if you were *my* daughter I would say you had fallen in love and that the affair was not going too happily."

Katherine looked at her with resentful admiration.

"All that?" she asked faintly.

"All that," Madame repeated firmly. "Now begin at the beginning and tell me all about it."

Katherine sighed thoughtfully.

"You're being very kind," she said at last, "but

I'm not sure that I want to talk about it."

"Because I am a friend of Chantal's," Madame completed for her. "You need not worry about that. Chantal is my neighbour, and my husband and I never quarrel with our neighbours. It is a rule of life we both have. But that doesn't mean that we necessarily approve of them, or even like them very much." She pushed Katherine's cup of coffee towards her and sat down opposite her, her clothes bespattered with distemper and her face completely innocent of any make-up. "Well?" she prompted.

Katherine found that once she had started on the story she couldn't stop. It came pelting, without any embellishments.

"I hate her," she said at last. "I hate her, and I've never hated anyone before!" And with that she burst into tears, and for some obscure reason felt a great deal better.

"But of course you don't hate her," Madame said briskly. "You are far too sensible to waste your energies doing any such thing. She leaves a bad taste in the mouth — in my mouth too! But to hate her? She is not worth the trouble."

Katherine smiled bleakly through her tears.

"It isn't exactly something that one can control," she objected.

Madame looked at her with approval.

"That is much better! Now, we shall see what can be done. First, I shall introduce you to my friends here, and you will be too busy to be anything else but gay and friendly. Then, after that, we shall think again. Where is Chantal now?"

"She's still at Sidi Behn Ahmed," Katherine told her.

Madame wrinkled up her forehead.

"Peter didn't mention her," she said doubtfully. "Still, it is not of the least importance."

Perhaps not to her! Katherine thought bitterly.

But it mattered to her! She knew exactly what the daily routine would be with Peter calling in every evening for a drink and a chat. In fact he probably called in a great deal more often than that with only Chantal there. And she quite simply couldn't bear to think about it.

"Why not?" she asked rather tearfully.

Madame looked first embarrassed and then determined.

"Because she is really a very boring topic of conversation," she said firmly, "and we have a great deal of painting still to do."

"Oh yes!" Katherine stood up immediately. "I'm so sorry. I've been keeping you from it, but if you give me a brush and some distemper I'd love to help."

"And so you shall!" Madame agreed warmly.

The more Katherine saw of the Verdons the more she liked them. They were as good as their word too about introducing her to all their friends, and she began to wonder why she had been so worried as to whether she would be accepted by the local people. More and more she became aware of the careful phrases and the polite silences when Chantal's name came up in the conversation, and she gradually became used to the idea that the French girl wasn't really very popular at all; more, that she was actively disliked by quite a number of her fellow countrymen who lived round about.

Katherine found that she was beginning to relax. She laughed more and she worried less. It had been years since she had had to take so little responsibility, and she made the most of it, enjoying her new freedom with a zest that half amused her in her saner moments because she knew that it was all really quite unlike her usual rather sober self. If Peter Kreistler could see her now he really would have reason for considering her a completely useless female. She had done nothing but please herself for days.

The bubble broke a few days after they had finished re-distempering the Verdon's house. Brahim came up to the house bringing the account books with him and also a short note in Arabic written in a very careful hand on cheap, lined notepaper.

"I brought this up from the Post Office for you," he said in his usual dignified manner. "Can you read it for yourself, or shall I do a translation for you?"

Katherine glanced at it curiously.

"I'm afraid I can't read any Arabic at all," she confessed. "In fact I can't think who could be writing to me in that language."

Brahim took the letter from her.

"It has been written by the letter-writer of Sidi Behn Ahmed for a woman named Lala."

Katherine flushed with pleasure.

"Lala!" she exclaimed. "What does she say? Has she had the baby yet?"

Brahim perused the short note with deliberate care.

"The baby is due," he said at last. "She asks that you should go down and be with her as you promised." He shook his head sadly. "Did you promise so rashly to do this thing?" he asked.

Katherine pulled the letter away from him, staring down at it, half hoping that by some miracle she would be able to read it for herself.

"Of course I promised! Lala helped me with a very difficult case, and after that she taught me Arabic. She's a *friend* of mine!"

Brahim's face crinkled up.

"It is too far to go for such a thing," he told her. "You would do better to telephone to the hospital and find out from the doctor if it is really necessary."

It was the sensible thing to do. Katherine could see that for herself. But she had become fond of

171

Lala and she had promised to be there — and if she went south she would see Peter again. It was funny how he had become Peter to her now. She hardly ever thought of him as Dr. Kreistler as she had schooled herself to do when she had worked for him for those few brief weeks.

"All right, I'll telephone," she agreed reluctantly. "I'll put through the call for this evening to make sure Dr. Kreistler will be there."

Brahim nodded approvingly.

"The doctor will tell you what you should do." He pulled his robes more closely round him and put the account book carefully down on the table. "Shall we begin with these?" he suggested quietly.

All through the day she would suddenly catch sight of the telephone and her mouth would go dry and her heart would start to hammer within her. It was nothing more than a bad attack of stage-fright, she told herself, for she wouldn't know what to say to the doctor, and he would think her a perfect fool for phoning!

But as the hour approached she felt more confident, and after a harassing half-hour with the various exchanges who were putting her through and seemed quite unable to understand a word she said, she felt positively ready for anything.

"May I speak to Dr. Kreistler, please?" she said to the nurse who took the call.

"Hold the line."

"This is a long-distance call," the exchange put in helpfully.

"I'll hurry, then," the nurse agreed enthusiastically, and in a few moments Katherine could hear the faint click of another receiver being picked up.

"Dr. Kreistler here."

He sounded so exactly like himself that she couldn't quite believe it. And she had been trying to persuade herself that she had been happy without him! She had never been so miserable in all her life.

"Hullo — Peter," she said weakly.

"Katherine!" The impatience had gone and she could distinctly hear the smile in his voice. So at least he was pleased to hear from her. "Is anything the matter?" he demanded. "Or is this just a social call?"

"N-neither. I had a letter from Lala."

"Did you?" She hadn't thought that his voice could sound so warm and comfortable.

"It was written by the official letter-writer of Sidi Behn Ahmed," she went on. "I hadn't realised that there were still such persons."

"Very important persons!" the doctor assured her. "And am I to know what the letter contained?"

Katherine pulled herself together with an effort. This was a most expensive call, and really she couldn't afford to waste the time in this silly way.

"She wants me to be there when she has her baby," she said briskly in her most professional tones. "I promised her that I would be there, you see," she added.

"So she told me," Peter said. "Are you coming?"

Katherine began to dither again.

"I don't know!" she confessed at last. "What do you think?"

He laughed. "I am being very naughty and teasing you just a little," he told her. "It would be too late for you to deliver the baby if you did come. Lala has already given birth to a son."

"To a son? Oh, she must be pleased!"

The doctor chuckled.

"She is pleased, her husband is pleased, and you sound pretty pleased yourself!"

"I'm delighted!" Katherine admitted simply. But somehow she didn't sound at all pleased after all. There was no reason for her to go down to Sidi

Behn Ahmed now, and she hadn't realised how much she had been looking forward to it, to getting back into harness and doing a real job of work. And she wanted to see Dr. Kreistler more than ever. She would be content, she thought, just to work with him. To see his strong competent hands dealing with his patients and to listen to his voice and to see him move.

"Are you still there, Katherine?" Peter asked. "Lala and her husband want you to name the child for them. Can you think of a name off-hand that I can tell them?"

She was immensely flattered.

"Oh, Peter, how nice of them!"

"And the name?" he prompted her with a touch of his old impatience.

Katherine heard the pips go, signifying the end of her allotted time on the wire.

"Tell them —" she began, and her voice broke slightly. "Tell them to name him after you," she said, and put down the receiver quickly before he could know that she was crying again. But it would be nice to think that somewhere on the edge of the great Sahara desert there was a little boy that had been called after Dr. Peter Kreistler.

CHAPTER TWELVE

ANOTHER letter came from Lala, this time written in the doctor's firm hand so that Katherine could read it for herself in English. It was a simple letter, stating that the boy had been duly called Peter and that she and her husband had been pleased with the choice. Try as she would, Katherine could see no personal references in it from Peter. It was rather a let-down after the way her heart had leapt when she had seen the envelope with his writing on it.

It was only later that she saw the postscript scrawled across the back of the paper:

Only five more days, Peter.

Only five more days to what? She counted them off on the calendar, and when the fifth day came she could hardly bring herself to go out. But Brahim quietly insisted that she should see the results of their digging up the water supply of the dying orchard. It was terribly hot away from the house, for the leafless trees afforded little protection from the blazing sun. Katherine climbed in and out of ditches and exchanged jokes with the weary labourers, who went on digging more or less mechanically no matter what the temperature was.

"I think it's here that the salt water is getting in," Brahim told her at last, pointing to a join in the pipes that looked quite indistinguishable from any other to Katherine.

"Can it be fixed?" she asked.

He nodded cheerfully.

"I think so. It is only a faulty join. We can try it and see if the trees improve."

Katherine looked at the fruit-trees all around her.

"They look completely dead to me," she said.

Brahim took out his knife and slashed at the bark of the nearest tree, revealing the soft wood underneath.

"The sap is still rising," he reported, "and the roots go deep."

Katherine wished she had brought her dark glasses with her. The rays of the sun were in her eyes and her head hurt. It was a black world covered with white glare and she felt slightly sick.

"I must get in out of the sun," she murmured. She gave the men a last smile and turned quickly, stumbling over the rough ground towards the gateway that led into the gardens. She paused there, hanging on to the gate and willing herself to recover.

"Sit down over here on this seat," a voice instructed her briskly, "and put your head down between your knees. Really, I am surprised that I should have to tell you something so simple!"

She did as he told her.

"Oh, Peter!" she gasped. The world began to right itself and the colours came back to the flowers in the garden. "Oh, Peter," she said again. "I meant to put on my prettiest dress and wash my hair just in case you came."

His strong hand pushed her head further down. "And why didn't you?" he asked.

"I wasn't sure you were coming," she said brokenly. "And I had to go and look at some trees of Brahim's."

He released his grasp on her and she was able to look up at him, to make sure that it really was him and not some dream of her own manufacture.

His eyes were amused, though his face was completely serious.

"Brahim's trees? I thought they were yours!"

She made a slight face at him and made to get up from the seat, but he pushed her gently back on

176

to it. Her hands tensed and she took a deep breath.

"Where's Chantal?" she asked.

He didn't even look particularly surprised that she should ask.

"She's outside, in the car."

Her eyes dropped.

"I see," she said.

He smiled.

"Do you? Are you sure?"

There was no need to answer him. She knew only too well that they had travelled up together, and they must have stopped somewhere for the night on the way or Chantal wouldn't be willing to stay in the car for an instant longer than she could help. No girl would! Perhaps they had even spent *two* nights on the way.

"Why doesn't she come in?" she asked crossly.

"Do you really want her to?" he countered.

"No," she admitted. "But she can't sit out in the car all day!"

He laughed delightedly.

"That's what I like best about you," he told her. "Your invariable calm good sense."

"You didn't always think so," she reminded him. How dared he? Calm good sense indeed! Surely she must have *some* more romantic qualities!

"My judgment was prejudiced," he admitted. "And for that I apologise."

She clenched her hands together.

"It doesn't matter," she said.

He reached down and took her hands into both of his.

"Shall we go and get Chantal out of the car?" he suggested. "She is not a very patient waiter."

It seemed to her that she didn't have any choice in the matter. She stood up and looked ruefully down at the trails of mud on her clothes. She would have liked to have slipped into the house and have changed her dress before coming face to face with the French girl. She could already imagine the way *she* would look, immaculate as ever and quite dazzlingly chic.

But for once Chantal looked quite ruffled. Her pale blue eyes were large and tired and there was a frail air about her that was quite new.

Katherine greeted her briefly, without touching her, and led the way slowly into the house.

"I'll order some cool drinks," she said.

Dr. Kreistler shook his head.

"Not for me." He turned to Chantal. "I shall come back for you in about an hour and take you to your train."

Chantal nodded and bit her lower lip.

"Whatever you say," she said indifferently.

The doctor bowed slightly to both girls and left the room. Katherine watched him go with a fatalistic feeling of approaching disaster.

"Will you have lemon or orange?" she asked.

"Lemon," said Chantal.

Katherine rang the bell and gave the order to the servant who hurried into the room to answer it. She had never quite got used to summoning people in this way and she sounded slightly apologetic as she asked for the two drinks. Chantal gave her a scornful look that made her seem much more familiar, and Katherine sat down abruptly on one of the chairs, realising once again how terribly hot it was and how her clothes were sticking to her back in the most uncomfortable way.

The lemon drinks arrived, the ice clinking against the tall glasses that stood on the tray together with a silver sugar bowl and two abnormally long-handled teaspoons to stir with.

"Did you have a good journey up?" Katherine asked.

Chantal's face was enigmatic, though she smiled slightly.

"I haven't been at Sidi Behn Ahmed," she said. "I've been staying in Tunis. Actually I left the day after you did." She shrugged her shoulders elaborately. "There was nothing to do there, was there? I can't imagine how you stood it so long all by yourself."

Katherine's mouth felt dry and she sipped her drink hastily.

"There is plenty for a nurse to do there. I wasn't lonely and I felt I was doing a worth-while job — or at least it could have been if someone did it on a more permanent basis."

"So Peter informed me," Chantal said dryly. "Twenty-four hours of how popular you were, how hard you worked, and how we had all misjudged you before you arrived were quite enough, let me tell you."

Katherine didn't attempt to hide her surprise.

"I expect it was," she said weakly.

"And so I made Beshir drive me up to Tunis," Chantal continued. "I didn't think you'd mind if I kept him to chauffeur me round for a bit. I hardly expected to be dug out of my hotel in the middle of the night and driven here so that I could have the pleasure of apologising to you for my sins! *That* was Peter's idea!"

Katherine swallowed hard.

"Apologise for what?" she said stupidly.

"I told him it wasn't necessary!" Chantal dismissed her contemptuously. "I don't suppose you even noticed that I didn't particularly like you. Why should you care?"

Katherine looked amused.

"I got a little worried when you started throwing scorpions around," she admitted, a little bewildered as to where all this was leading.

179

Chantal's pale blue eyes flickered over her.

"How English you are!" she said with icy dislike. "The brave front, but the womanly tears when there is a man's shoulder to cry on! Very well, I admit you have won, Nurse Katherine Lane, but I shall never be sorry for anything I have said or done to you. Is that clear?"

"Perfectly."

Chantal turned on her viciously.

"That's what I hate about you!" she exclaimed fiercely. "You never say anything. Why don't you tell me that you hate me too?"

"Because it wouldn't be true," Katherine said thoughtfully. "I thought it was for some time, but then I was made to realise it simply wasn't worth the trouble." She faced the French girl fearlessly. "I had never met anyone like you before I came to Tunisia, you see. I thought that everyone else would admire the way you dressed as much as I did, and that they wouldn't notice the unkind things you said to people whom you didn't think mattered. But I was wrong. I found that they had noticed and that they didn't particularly care. Why should they? They didn't have to live with you. But they didn't like you for it. Somehow it didn't seem nearly so bad when I realised that everyone else had seen through you too."

"How dare you?" Chantal spat at her. "How dare you?"

Katherine smiled at her. For the first time in her relationship with Chantal she felt completely master of the situation.

"Well, you did ask," she said. "Shall we talk about something more pleasant now? Where are you and Peter going when he comes back for you?"

Chantal looked furtively up through her eyelashes.

"Ah! Wouldn't you like to know? But I'll leave you to guess. At least Peter will be driving *me!* And how you wish it were you, don't you, little Miss Clever?"

Katherine blenched.

"Yes, I do," she admitted. "I don't think, after all, that we have anything more to say to one another, have we? I think I'll go up to my room." She went out of the room with her head held high, but turned again as she reached the foot of the stairs. "I hope you'll make Peter very happy," she said tightly.

Chantal smiled silkily.

"I shall!" she said.

The Arab boy had closed the shutters in Katherine's room and it was almost in total darkness when she entered it. She threw herself down on the bed and wished she had an electric fan in the ceiling like the ones downstairs. Surely it was impossible for it to get any hotter. The perspiration ran down her face, ruining her make-up, and she heard the first, distant sounds of thunder in the sky. It was going to rain! She could hardly believe it. She had never seen any rain in Tunisia. She tried to imagine the *wadis* as fast-running rivers, but they obstinately remained the dried-up river beds she had seen all down the countryside.

She ran to the window and opened it wide, hoping to catch a flash of the lightning as it ripped through the sky. It would be wonderful to feel the rain on her face and be cool again, and it would be so good for the fruit-trees as well. Perhaps it would save those poor, dying trees as she couldn't believe anything else would.

There was another flash of lightning followed by a crash of thunder that was close enough to be frightening. She turned away from the window and glanced round the now sunlit room. Standing in the middle of the floor was a small pale blue basket, filled to the brim with oddments and crowned with an ornamental five-branch candle. It was one of the marriage baskets she had seen in the *souks*. For a long moment she stared down at it, wondering how on earth it could have got there. A marriage basket! For *her?*

Her hands were trembling as she took the things out of it and laid them in a row on the floor in front of her. There was a nightdress and négligée that made Chantal's look cheap. How had he known about that? she wondered. And a number of different coloured veils that would be ideal for her to wear in the desert. And a couple of boxes of dates identical to the one she had once bought but had never had the courage to offer to him.

She could hear sounds of movement downstairs, but she didn't stir. She didn't need to say goodbye to Chantal. Peter would take her to wherever it was she was going and then he would come back. Her eyes took in every detail of the intricate plaiting of the coloured papers that were woven round the five-branched candle. A Tunisian bride would light it on her wedding night and would know that it was keeping the "evil eye" away —

And then he would come back!

Galvanised into sudden action, she tore the pins out of her hair, shook it free so that it cascaded down behind her shoulders, and disappeared into the beautifully appointed bathroom that led off her room.

The dress she chose was not the newest in her wardrobe, but it was a firm favourite, showing off the fairness of her hair to advantage and making her feel at her most attractive. She gazed at herself in the looking-glass for a long moment, wondering whether to put her hair up again or to let it fly free with no more than an Alice band to hold it off her face. She looked younger with it down and more uncertain, but it suited her too in a way that the other style never had. It wasn't so efficient, or even very practical, but Peter had said that he liked it down. She smiled at herself and her reflection smiled back at her. So she had, after all, washed her hair and put on her prettiest dress.

She heard the car coming up the drive through the now heavy rain. It wasn't the Land Rover. It was a much lighter car and the engine was spluttering as though it would like to stall but didn't quite dare. The rain must have got into the sparking plugs, Katherine thought. She could imagine it, pouring down from a slate-grey sky and drenching everything beneath it.

She turned on the lights to make the room more cheerful, and they flickered nervously before they came on to their full strength as though they too were a little afraid of the thunder that still rumbled ominously overhead.

Although she was expecting him, it still came as a shock to her when Dr. Kreistler entered the room. She spun round to greet him, but the words died on her lips. He had discarded his mackintosh, but little drops of water flashed like diamonds in his hair and his shoes and socks were soaking wet.

"W-would you like to change?" she asked him abruptly.

He looked impatiently down at his feet.

"Perhaps I'd better," he sighed. "I seem to be leaving marks on your beautifully polished floors.

"That — that wasn't why I suggested it," she said, and blinked at him. The trouble was, she thought, that neither of them knew where to begin.

"Wasn't it?"

She went over to him and gave him a slight push towards a chair, going down on her knees to take them off for him.

"Oh, no, you don't!" he said firmly. "I'm quite capable of taking off my own shoes. If you want to be helpful, you can look in my bag in the hall and find a spare pair."

She went without a word. He had put his suitcase neatly in a corner together with his medical bag. It was large and shabby and she thought that he must have brought it out of Hungary with him. The locks were stiff and hurt her fingers and he had packed so badly that it was impossible to find anything in it. She scrabbled around in one corner and came up with a single sock that needed darning anyway.

"I suppose you did pack some spare shoes?" she called out to him.

He padded over to her in his bare feet.

"How should I know?" he asked her impatiently. "I was in a hurry. I only caught the plane by the skin of my teeth." He knelt down beside her. "Here, let me have a look," he said.

He was so close that she could feel the warmth of his body against her bare arm. Against her will she coloured slightly. He sat back on his heels and put out a hand to touch her hair, feeling for the places that were still slightly damp.

"Have you been out in the rain?" he asked.

She shook her head, wondering that her own knees should have turned to water.

"Of course not!" she said tartly.

He smiled slightly, looking pleased with himself. "So you did wash it after all," he said.

She nodded, completely unable to say anything. With a quick movement she jumped to her feet and went back into the other room. She could hear the brisk tap of her heels against the polished tiles and felt like kicking them off so that she would be as barefoot as he. He came after her, a pair of shoes in one hand and his dry socks in the other.

"And you've been upstairs?" he prompted her.

She blushed vividly, the hot colour rushing up her cheeks.

"Yes," she said.

He stood for a moment watching her, and then he sat down and began to put on his shoes and socks.

"And it *is* a very pretty dress!" he said almost nonchalantly. He tied the second lace with neat, competent fingers and looked up at her, his eyes filled with laughter. "I love you," he said.

She raised her head a couple of inches. I know, she wanted to say, I saw a basket upstairs; but what actually came out was:

"Where did Chantal go?"

His eyebrows rose, giving him a quizzical expression.

"I thought you'd ask that," he chuckled.

"Why?" she demanded, a little hurt that he should find her so amusing.

"Because —" He paused, choosing his words with care. "Because you are probably the most feminine person I have ever met," he went on more slowly. "What do you want to know about Chantal, my love?"

She put a hand up to her hair and was mildly surprised to find it hanging down her back instead of in its more usual neat plaits.

"I'm not being vulgarly curious," she told him. "I know you — you liked her —" The words twisted her tongue and she came, helplessly, to a halt. "She said you were going with her!" she burst out.

He didn't attempt to touch her.

"What exactly do you want to know?" he repeated.

She wanted to know so many things. Her mind went back to the *souk* in Tunis and Chantal saying, "I buy all my perfume here. Peter gave me the first lot and it has become a tradition now." And all those many, many other implications that she and Peter were more than friends.

"I want to know where she has gone," she said simply.

"She has gone to visit a friend of hers in Oran."
He looked down at his neatly manicured hands. "I
rather fancy that she will find it more convenient
not to return to Tunisia. There is nothing here for
her any more. There is no reason why you should
continue to support her. In fact you should never
have been allowed to get yourself into that position
in the first place! Besides, I fancy you will have
little need of the estate at Hammamet in the future.
I think it would be a pleasant gesture to give it to
the government so that it can be divided up amongst
people who would make good use of the land."

Katherine gave a little gasp.

"Can I do that?" she asked. "And what about
Sidi Behn Ahmed?"

He nodded approvingly.

"That also," he agreed. "We can keep a few hec-
tares of land for our own use, but as for the rest it
will be a nuisance. We have other work to do."

She bit her lip to hide a smile. He had the whole
of their future buttoned up, it seemed.

"We?" she asked him gently.

"We!" he agreed firmly. He stood up and pulled
her into his arms, looking down straight into her
eyes. "I'm afraid I'm not doing this very well," he
said humbly, "but then, you see, I have never pro-
posed to anyone before."

She buried her face into his shoulder.

"You haven't now!" she teased him.

She could feel him laughing against her.

"Indeed I have! I have gone further," he retorted, "I have even brought you the wedding presents!"

Her eyes mocked him gently.

"I know," she said. "I found them upstairs. Oh,
Peter, you should have *said* something! I thought you
were in love with Chantal and were glad to have her
to yourself when I came back here. I was so miser-

able that even Madame Verdon was worried about me!"

"So she told me. My foolish love, did you really think I could prefer anyone else after I had got to know you?"

"Yes, I did!" she assured him.

"But not any longer?"

She shook her head, and a new urgency came into his hands as he drew her closer, kissing her first on the mouth and then her eyes and her hair and her mouth again until they were both breathless.

"It is terrible that you should have been unhappy," he said at last. "But I had first to make sure that Chantal would follow her brother's so excellent example and leave us in peace. That was soon done, but then I was stuck down in the south until I could find someone who would stand in for me. Tomorrow we must catch the plane back to Gafsa. That's all the time I have. We shall be married in Sidi Behn Ahmed, yes?"

"Yes," she said meekly. "Oh, Peter, I love you so much."

He smiled.

"But you must be quite sure, my love," he insisted gently. "I am twice a foreigner to you. I am a Hungarian refugee who has taken Tunisian nationality. There will be few English people for you to talk to."

"There will be you," she said.

"Is that enough for you?"

"It's everything!" she told him frankly. "That and the opportunity to work with you."

He kissed her again.

"I will make you very happy," he promised her. "As happy as you are beautiful," he added, running his hands through her long fair hair. "Beloved," he whispered.

Sidi Behn Ahmed was *en fête*. The whole oasis turned out to watch as the German priest arrived from the nearby mission to marry Dr. Kreistler and the nurse from England whom they had come to love.

Lala sat in the courtyard of Katherine's house unashamedly suckling her young son.

"Why has no one put up the marriage tent for you?" she asked.

It took time for Katherine to understand the question, and when she did she was very little wiser.

"Is it usual?" she asked.

Lala nodded her head positively.

"For the first week of marriage it is good to be alone," she said. "People come to congratulate the bride during the day, but at night there is no one but you and your husband."

Katherine put the finishing touches to her dress.

"Dr. Kreistler is coming here," she said. "It's nicer than his house and there's more room."

Lala thought about this information for a few minutes and then smiled with approval.

"I go now," she said. "We are all feasting tonight."

For Katherine the ceremony came and went in a dream. She exchanged her vows with Peter as though it was the most natural thing in the world to do, and then she sat opposite him at the table as they entertained the priest to dinner. Ali had cooked the dinner to perfection and the priest had brought a bottle of wine from the cellars of his Order to grace the occasion.

But at last that too was over and they went to see him off in his ancient jeep that had been bought from the American army after the war, and they were alone.

A ring of fires showed through the date-palms of the oasis and there was a general air of expectancy all about them. Katherine led the way into the house and turned into her husband's arms.

"Are you happy?" she asked him.

He kissed her for answer, and she knew she had no need to ask again. There was a new note that had been sounded between them and they were no longer two people but only one.

"Shall we light the candle?" he asked in her ear.

She nodded, and together they lit the five wicks of the marriage-candle he had given her. She took it to the window and placed it in the silver candlestick that waited for it there. Outside, the people looked up and saw it. It is well, they said, and went back to their own affairs.

Each month from Harlequin

8 NEW FULL LENGTH ROMANCE NOVELS

Listed below are the latest three months' releases:

ALL BOOKS 60c

These titles are available at your local bookseller, or through the Harlequin Reader Service, M.P.O. Box 707, Niagara Falls, N.Y. 14302; Canadian address 649 Ontario St., Stratford, Ont.

A

FREE!
Harlequin Romance Catalogue

Here is a wonderful opportunity to read many of the Harlequin Romances you may have missed.

The HARLEQUIN ROMANCE CATALOGUE lists hundreds of titles which possibly are no longer available at your local bookseller. To receive your copy, just fill out the coupon below, mail it to us, and we'll rush your catalogue to you!

Following this page you'll find a sampling of a few of the Harlequin Romances listed in the catalogue. Should you wish to order any of these immediately, kindly check the titles desired and mail with coupon.

Have You Missed Any of These
Harlequin Romances?

All books are 60c. Please use the handy order coupon.

X